The Plague

The Plague

MICKEY SMITH

RESOURCE *Publications* · Eugene, Oregon

THE PLAGUE

Resource Publications
An Imprint of Wipf and Stock Publishers
199 W. 8th Ave., Suite 3
Eugene, OR 97401

www.wipfandstock.com

PAPERBACK ISBN: 978-1-6667-3636-6
HARDCOVER ISBN: 978-1-6667-9453-3
EBOOK ISBN: 978-1-6667-9454-0

JANUARY 14, 2022 3:20 PM

CHAPTER ONE

I T's eerie how disasters happen on days that are calm and almost unremarkable. Such was the case back in the early twentieth century for a city in Japan.

Over 400 children went to Honkawa Elementary School in Hiroshima, Japan while adults went to work. It was a day just like any other day until "Little Boy" came to town.

In that one day over one hundred thousand Japanese men, women, and children lost their lives.

Today was destined to be another day of tragedy like that day in Japan many, many years ago. Only today would be a day of worldwide tragedy.

This day started all over the world just like any other day. In China, people would be finishing up their day in a few hours and heading home while in the central USA it was 6:30 the next morning.

Mike Reynolds was having his first cup of coffee sitting down at his kitchen table in Avondale, Georgia, located just a few miles east of Atlanta. He and his wife Julie bought this home a little more than five years ago, located in a quiet neighborhood in what he considered the perfect location. He was an EMT and worked for a company called Life Express in Atlanta, so living in Avondale put him close enough to work without having to live in Atlanta proper.

Life Express operated differently than most ambulance companies. Where most companies worked on a schedule where their EMTs would work twenty-four to forty-eight hours at a time and then have forty-eight hours off, Life Express put their people on rotating eight-hour shifts that would run a week at a time.

This week, Mike was on third shift, which ran from eleven at night to seven the next morning. Most companies called that a graveyard shift, but the people at Life Express refused to do that. Being in the profession of saving lives, no one could bring themselves to call it that, so they just called it third shift.

Mike's wife, Julie, came into the kitchen just as he was putting his coffee cup down on the table. She leaned over and gave him a kiss.

"Good morning, Baby," she said.

He smiled at her and said, "It is now."

"Sarah called last night, and she's going to come over and have dinner with us tonight," Julie told him. Sarah was their twenty-year-old daughter who was currently in college and had been living on her own for almost a year.

"Awesome. It's been too long since we've seen her."

"Yeah, I know. I mean, today is already Tuesday, and we haven't seen her since we were at church Sunday. That's almost three days. I don't know how we've survived," Julie said with a smirk.

"Laugh all you want, but she's our only child and I'm still having to adjust to this new phase of life."

At the same time in downtown Atlanta, columnist Paige Summers was waking up to a slightly different theme.

"The sun's up Aunt Paige! It's time to get our day started!" Paige's niece, Lilly, yelled while jumping up and down on her bed. Paige's sister Amanda stood in the bedroom doorway with a smirk on her face and a cup of coffee in her hand.

Paige reached over to one of the pillows and covered her face. Speaking through the pillow with a muffled voice, she said, "Go away, Lilly. I'm hibernating." She reached over and felt where Lilly was and tickled her in the ribs. Lilly squealed with laughter.

Amanda spoke up. "Okay, Lilly, let's go get some breakfast while Aunt Paige gets up. Paige, I'll have you a cup of coffee sitting on the breakfast table, so don't take too long or it'll get cold." Lilly and her mom left the room and Paige rolled over on her stomach.

Amanda had moved in with Paige when she was pregnant with Lilly. She had just found out that her boyfriend had been cheating on her and wanted to sever all ties with him. Moving in with her sister seemed like a good answer for them both. Lilly was now five years old, and the boyfriend had been out of the picture since before Lilly was born. The arrangement worked out well for both sisters. With both of them working, they were able to afford a bigger apartment in a nicer neighborhood. It's difficult for anyone who's a single parent in Atlanta to make ends meet, but with both incomes, they were able to get along comfortably.

Paige was a journalist for a local magazine while Amanda was a nurse at Piedmont Hospital.

After a few minutes, Paige got out of bed, put on her robe, and walked into the kitchen where, as promised, a cup of coffee was waiting for her.

This was part of Paige's normal morning routine. After coffee and breakfast, Paige would go to work while Amanda stayed home with Lilly. After Paige got home, they almost always ate together, and then Amanda would head to the hospital while Paige watched Lilly.

"So, what's up at the magazine for you today?" Amanda asked Paige during breakfast.

"My latest column about the corruption with the election process should be back from the editor this morning. So, most of my morning will be spent sprucing it up before I send it out for production, and then I'll start researching my next story."

Paige was one of those rare people who truly enjoyed what she did for a living. It wasn't just a job-- it was something she felt compelled to do.

Back at Mike's house, the day was beginning to get started for real. Mike decided to cut the grass while his wife Julie went to the grocery store to get some things for the evening's dinner.

The house had what Mike called a postage-stamp yard that was about a quarter of an acre. At that size, Mike could not bring himself to buy a riding mower, as most of his neighbors had done. Instead, he used a push mower that he kept in a metal shed in the backyard along with other tools. He always started with the mower on the bulk of the yard, and then when that was done, he would move to the gas-powered trimmer for the edges.

Julie had left for the grocery store before he got started, and by the time he had moved to the trimmer, he saw her car pulling back in the drive-way. It took him less than an hour to get the trimming done, and as soon as he stepped out of the tool shed, he saw Julie sitting at the patio table with a large glass of iced tea waiting for him.

He smiled and walked over to where she was. "So, what did you and Sarah decide for dinner tonight?"

"I'm making homemade pizza and Sarah is bringing over cheesecake. And what are your plans for the rest of the day?"

He took a sip of tea. It felt good going down. "I've got some more things to get done around the house today. Once I'm done, I figure to take a shower and then maybe take a nap before Sarah gets here. It always takes me a couple of nights to get acclimated to the third shift for some reason."

"That's because God designed us to be diurnal and not nocturnal. This shift goes against His natural order. It's a good thing they give you three days off between shifts, so you can re-acclimate yourself!"

The rest of the day went pretty much the way Mike expected it to go. Once he laid down for his nap, he could feel himself getting tired. Even though this was the first night of the third shift for him, he was so used to the routine that he naturally started to feel drowsy and was ready for a nap.

Mike hadn't been in bed more than ten minutes before he dozed off to sleep. Then what felt like just a moment later but was almost three hours later, he woke to the sound of Julie and Sarah talking down the hall in the living room. Not wanting to have to change clothes later, Mike went ahead on put on his Life Express uniform and walked into the living room.

Beth noticed him walking down the hallway.

"Hi, Baby. Did you have a good nap?"

"I think so. It's always a challenge getting used to third shift." Then he walked over and kissed Sarah on the forehead. "Hi, baby girl."

Beth handed him a cup of coffee and said, "Sarah's going to hang out with me tonight while you're at work. We're going to have a movie night."

"That sounds like a plan. Maybe you could start with one I would enjoy before I have to go to work."

With that, Sarah smiled and offered, "We're already ahead of you on that one. A few years ago, Jim Caviezel starred in a remake of 'The Count of Monte Cristo.' How's that one sound to you?"

"I'm in." he said with a smile.

Julie smiled and said, "First things first though. The timer will go off in about fifteen minutes letting us know that the pizza is done so we can have dinner, then I'm looking forward to a slice of that cheesecake Sarah brought over."

At the same time, Paige, Amanda, and Lilly were having a meal together after Paige got home from work and before Amanda headed off to the hospital for her shift. Amanda had made ravioli, one of Lilly's favorites. They had celebrated Lilly's birthday the week before and the decorations were still up because Lilly had begged for them to not be taken down.

"Lilly, we're going to have to clean up these decorations." Paige said as she pushed a balloon out of her way. It had fallen from the ceiling onto the table.

"Can we do it tomorrow morning?" Lilly asked.

"I'll get it cleaned up myself while you're at work tomorrow," Amanda offered.

Paige smiled and said, "Thanks."

Then without any other talk about the decorations, they enjoyed a quiet dinner, completely unaware that this would be their last meal together.

Meanwhile, Mike, Julie, and Sarah finished their dinner and eased into the living room to relax and enjoy a movie together.

"How's everything with you and Chet?" Julie asked Sarah as they sat down.

Sarah had been seeing Chet for almost a year now. He was a couple of years older than Sarah and was finishing up his Master's degree in theology.

Mike had to admit that Chet seemed like a great guy, and it was obvious that Sarah had fallen head over heels for him. The one thing that gave him pause about this relationship was that Chet had made it known that he intended to be a missionary. Mike could see that this relationship was becoming a permanent one, and he wasn't so sure about how he felt about his daughter being the wife of a missionary. He knew that she could end up in some pretty sketchy places.

"They're going great. As a matter of fact, I think he would like to talk to you and Dad about something sometime this week."

"Well, your Dad is just starting third shift tonight, so Chet would need to come over between six and ten in the evening."

Sarah smiled and said, "Thanks. I'll let him know, and we can set something up."

Mike truly didn't know what to say, so he didn't say anything and just hoped the moment would pass, and it did.

The rest of the evening went smoothly. Julie made some popcorn and the three of them sat and watched "The Count of Monte Cristo".

When the movie ended, it was time for Mike to head to work. He kissed the girls goodnight and told them not to stay up binge-watching horror movies, adding that he would like to get some sleep when the shift was over. Then he laughed at his own joke, knowing they were bound to watch some chick-flicks.

CHAPTER TWO

MIKE pulled into the employee parking area of Life Express almost thirty minutes before the shift started. Ever since he was young Mike had developed the habit of being early for everything. It was a habit that had been passed down to him from his father and as far as he was concerned it was a habit that needed to be taught to a lot of the younger generation. The other members of his team also had a habit of making it to their shift before time to start which always made the start of each shift smooth.

When he walked toward the garage, he noticed that one of the trucks was out on a run and the other two were sitting quietly in the garage. Each shift was made up of three crews and two dispatchers. Being the one with the most experience, Mike was the team leader, which meant that he would get the rundown from the previous shift. That way he was made aware of the equipment lists of each truck and could make sure that they all had the right supplies.

Dave Banks came out of the break room, saw Mike, and headed towards him. Dave was Mike's counterpart from the team he would be relieving.

"Hi Dave, how's the night gone so far?"

Dave had a quizzical look on his face when he answered, "It's been unusually slow tonight, but I'm not gonna complain."

"Odds are that the lull in activity will be over and we'll have an extra busy shift tonight," Mike said.

"That's normally the way it works out," Dave answered.

"So, let's go sit down for a minute and you can get me up to speed on what's needed for shift change."

The two of them walked into the breakroom and Dave proceeded to catch Mike up to speed on the shift. All the trucks were fully equipped and were ready to go. While the two of them were going over everything, the rest of the members of Mike's team arrived. Joey Lund, the newest and youngest member of the team, was partnered with Donna Moore. She was a good partner for Joey because she had more than five years of experience and Mike felt she would be a good mentor for Joey. Another team was Alter Cagan and Lisa Stokes. They were both very good at their jobs and worked well together. Mike teamed himself up with Allen Majors, the class clown of the group, not because he felt like he needed the comedy routine, but because he felt that if anyone could keep Allen reigned in, it would be him.

Not long after Joey started with them did Mike see that he had done the right thing. Joey was an outspoken Christian. Not that he was ever in people's face, but he just didn't hide who he was. One day he started to invite everyone to a revival that was going on at his church. The girls were noncommittal while Alter said he would not make it because he was a Jew. Allen, with a loud laugh, chimed in, "Why aren't you wearing a he-jab?" For his part Alter did not lose his cool he just smiled and said, "The Hijab is a head covering worn by Muslim women. I believe what you are referring to is known as the Kippah, which is worn by orthodox Jews. I am what's known as a reform or Liberal Jew. We see the head covering as optional."

That short conversation alone made Mike glad he had assigned himself to be partnered with Allen.

With the briefing now over and the third truck coming back in, the shift looked like it was going to switch over seamlessly. Each set of partners went to their truck and started checking everything out to make sure it would be ready at a second's notice.

Just then Allen walked over to Joey with a serious look on his face. "Hey Joey, could I talk to you for a minute?"

Without turning their heads everyone on the team switched their focus to Allen and Joey. Joey suggested that they go sit in the break room and the two of them walked off.

"I'm not so sure that's a good idea, letting the two of them go off alone like that. I mean the two of them are like night and day," Lisa said.

Mike was wondering the same thing when Alter uncharacteristically spoke up. "I think we should leave them alone for a bit. Allen seemed very serious, like something was troubling him. Somehow we all instinctively know who we should turn to when something is bothering us, and for Allen, that person may be Joey."

"Alter may be right. I've got to admit, Allen did look very serious-- not his normal joking self. Let's all finish checking out the trucks and give them some time," Mike said, and then went back to what he had been doing. The others followed his lead.

Within thirty minutes the bell started to ring and the dispatcher's voice came over the loudspeaker. "We need all crews on this. A bus full of passengers just crashed through the window of a pub, and we've got multiple injuries."

With that, everyone ran to their respective trucks-- everyone except Allen and Joey. The truck with Alter and Lisa was the first to head out, while Mike was waiting on Allen and Donna was waiting for Joey. Without saying anything, the two of them jumped out of their trucks and sprinted to the break room. When they walked in, they were completely unprepared for what they found. Both Allen and Joey were collapsed at the table. With a quick check of their vitals, Mike and Donna knew that both men were dead.

Donna started to cry, and then Mike's years of experience and the urgency of the call took over.

"We've got to keep moving. For now, come with me in my truck and we can radio Anthony to let him know what's happened. Right now, some people need us."

Without saying another word, Donna and Mike went to his truck. Mike fired it up and pulled out. The dispatcher had already sent the address of the call right to the GPS of the truck, so Mike followed the GPS, while Donna got on the radio with Anthony the dispatcher to let him know about Allen and Joey.

Once they got to the scene, the first thing they saw was the nose of a bus sticking into a restaurant. It was as if the bus driver passed out and the bus crashed right through the plate glass window of the pub, never hitting the brakes. Witnesses said that at least four people were sitting at a table by the window when the bus hit. It was believed that all four of them were under the bus.

Mike and Donna were almost five minutes behind Alter and Lisa when they got to the scene. Lisa had worked her way under the bus by crawling on her stomach.

Alter saw Mike and Donna come in and instantly a questioning look was on his face.

"I'll explain later. What have we got?"

Just then Lisa's voice could be heard from under the bus. "Four dead."

"Everybody off the bus?" Mike asked.

"Yeah, but there were three dead on the bus and none of them had any injuries. Plus the driver- he's dead also. No explanations."

Some other people had injuries but nothing major. Donna treated two people with cuts from flying glass while Mike explained the episode at the station. Just then their radios went off with more calls. Mike got on the radio and said that Alter and Lisa had to wait for the coroner at their current location, but that he and Donna would head out right away.

The second call was from a young guy in his late teens. It seemed that he had just arrived home to find the door locked, and his parents did not respond to his banging on their bedroom window. He managed to get the window open and crawled through it to find both of his parents unconscious in their bed. Not able to get either of them to respond, he called 911.

Mike and Donna got there as quickly as they could, but all they could do was to call the coroner and wait at the scene. The young man on the scene broke down instantly, and neither Mike nor Donna could do anything to help him calm down.

That was always the hardest part of the job- dealing with the grief of people who had just lost their loved ones and not knowing how to console them.

The rest of the night was a whirlwind for the crews. Calls came on top of each other. They sent as many calls as they could to other services. The trouble was, all the EMT services were overwhelmed with calls. There were car wrecks and people collapsing on their jobs. The entire emergency system was overwhelmed. By the time they got to their third call, Mike got word over the radio from Anthony that the normal routine was going to be changed. Normally, an EMT did not officially pronounce someone dead on the scene. They had to wait for the coroner to do that. However, tonight the coroners were so overwhelmed that they could not get to the scenes very quickly and the EMTs were having to wait, not able to go on their next call. Anthony radioed Mike and told him that he had gotten word from the coroners' office that the EMTs could put a black tag on the dead bodies and then go to their next call without waiting for the coroner to arrive.

By the time the shift ended all four of them were exhausted both physically and mentally. Once they got back to the station Mike asked Anthony if there was any news on the cause of the deaths of Joey and Allen.

"No word yet. The hospitals are just as overwhelmed as we've been, and Justin is here for a briefing from you so his team can take over."

At six-thirty in the morning, Paige woke up. The apartment was surprisingly quiet. It had not been all that quiet during the night with all the ambulances driving by. Amanda wouldn't be home yet for another forty-five minutes, and Lilly had most likely been kept up just like she had been with all the noise.

"Let her sleep," Paige thought to herself, as she got up and headed towards the kitchen to make some coffee. She had barely got the coffee made and sat down to a cup when Amanda came bursting in with a frazzled look on her face. She saw Paige sitting at the table, and a look of relief swept over her face.

"Thank God you're OK."

"What's wrong honey?"

Amanda came and sat down at the table next to her. "Something's going on, and it seems worse than the pandemic ever was." She paused as if she didn't know how to explain what she had been witnessing at the hospital. "We've been dealing with it all night at the hospital. People have been dying for no reason all night long all over the city. We tried calling another hospital to help and then found out that they were just as swamped as we were." Then suddenly she looked around and another look of panic came on her expression. "Where's Lilly?"

"I let her sleep in because the ambulances kept going all night last night..."

"LILLY!"

She yelled, interrupting Paige in mid-sentence. She got up and ran to Lilly's room.

Paige had barely gotten to her feet when she heard her sister's screams from the bedroom. Amanda ran down the hall carrying Lilly. "Call Piedmont and tell them we are coming in now!"

They rushed to the hospital with Paige driving and Amanda in the back with Lilly giving her mouth to mouth. Once they got to the hospital, an emergency team met them at the door and took over with Lilly. Ten minutes later, Amanda's world came crashing down when they pronounced Lilly dead.

Mike just wanted to get home and wrap his arms around his wife. He knew Julie and Sarah would have breakfast waiting when he got there, and it comforted him to be leaving this insanity. By the time he pulled into the driveway, the tension from the night before was already starting to work its way out of his nerves.

He walked in through the kitchen door and was surprised not to see anyone in the kitchen. He looked around and noticed that nothing in there had been touched. There were skillets on the stove and no dishes on the table.

"Julie, Sarah!" he called but got no answer.

The tinges of dread started to creep up on him, but he fought those off. Those were just leftover emotions from the horrible night he had just gone through. He saw a flicker of light out of the corner of his eye and realized it was the TV in the other room. He walked into the living room and a sense of relief washed over him as he looked in and saw Sarah curled up in the love seat and Julie on the couch. The flicker he had seen was the end credits of a movie they had obviously fallen asleep watching. He saw the remote sitting on the love seat, so he picked it up and turned off the TV. Then he whispered, "Good morning baby girl." He bent over and kissed her forehead.

As soon as his lips touched her forehead, his heart stopped and his blood froze. Sarah's skin was cold. Feeling waves of panic, he tried to find a pulse, but there was none. He instinctively went to Julie. She was also gone. In that one instant, Mike's entire world had been ripped away from him.

CHAPTER THREE

THE plague was a global incident. There wasn't a place on earth that had not been affected. In the U.S., almost twenty percent of the population had been wiped out. Funeral homes all across the country were overwhelmed, not able to adequately handle the volume of deaths that had hit the country, but also trying to manage their own crippling losses as well. In some cases, hospitals and morgues had bodies with no one to claim them. Because of the overwhelming volume, it was decided that bodies would be cremated and the ashes would be passed on to whomever came to claim them. The entire process of dealing with the sudden deaths took months, all because of what happened in just one day.

Paige Summer was one of those who were left to pick up the pieces after the plague hit. Paige's sister, Amanda, couldn't live with the loss of her daughter and within a week of her daughter's death, Amanda became one of the thousands of suicides that became another result of the plague.

Paige found herself as part of a vast faceless crowd, one of many who found themselves walking through life with no purpose beyond the agonizing need to find a reason for what had happened.

Paige believed everything in life had a reason or at least a cause, and something deep within her was not going to let her stop without finding some answers. Her job as a columnist provided her with enough contacts to at least get started.

For Paige it wasn't even a conscious decision, it was just something she had to do. She had to find out what had happened and she didn't care how dark an alley she had to go down, as long as she found out the truth.

The obvious beginning would have been to talk to people in the medical field, but her instincts made her start with talking to people in medical research. After a few calls, she got an appointment with a doctor at the Center for Medical Research in Atlanta.

Upon arriving at the Center, she was surprised by how expansive it was. The campus, as they called it, looked at first glance more like a major university than what she had expected of a research center. Her appointment with Dr. Lauren Parks was at 10 a.m. and by habit, she was almost ten minutes early. That was a trait that she had picked up from her father. He had always told her, "If you are scheduled to start work by eight and you don't arrive until eight, then you're late."

The Center had one obvious main entrance, so she parked her car in the parking lot nearest to that and walked in. Walking through the double electric doors into a breezeway made the entrance much like that of a hospital. Once through the entrance, there was a reception desk with a young man sitting behind the counter, talking to an attractive young black woman. Paige walked up to introduce herself.

"Hello, my name is Paige Summers and…" She barely got the words out before the young lady spoke to her.

"You're early. I like that. Come this way." The lady smiled as she held out her hand. They shook hands briefly, and the lady turned to lead Paige down a hallway. She was wearing peach-colored scrubs, so Paige thought she must have been an assistant who worked with Dr. Parks. They turned into the door that was labeled, "Lauren Parks."

Paige was surprised when the young woman walked over and sat behind the desk. "So what exactly did you want to talk with me about, Ms. Summers?"

Paige stammered a little in response. "You're Dr. Parks?"

Lauren Parks smiled at the columnist. "So, am I too young or too black?"

"Well, you are younger than I expected."

If anything, the smile on the woman's face brightened. "Thank you." Then without wasting a breath she turned the conversation to the reason for their appointment. "My assistant tells me you are going to write an article about the plague and you were looking for some input from the Center. What sort of input are you looking for?"

She wanted to scream out the question, *Why did my niece die?* but the journalist in her didn't allow it. "I'm looking for something that may explain what happened and for some kind of evidence to show we may be able to prevent it from ever happening again."

Dr. Parks leaned back in her chair slightly and looked at Paige for a second, then broke eye contact and looked down at the desk before she spoke again. "I'm sorry Ms. Summers, but I'm afraid you've come to the wrong place. I don't have any answers to give you."

Paige could tell by the doctor's body language that she knew something, and either she wasn't willing to talk, or Paige had not asked the right question, so she tried a different angle. "There were tens of thousands of victims here in the Atlanta Metro area alone and since this is the only research facility in the area, I know that this facility either helped with the research or was a hub for other research centers. Either way, a lot of information has passed through these halls." Paige paused briefly to see if her words were having any effect. She could see the doctor's facial expression soften almost imperceptibly. "Tell me, Dr. Parks, did you lose someone to the plague?"

A somber look came across her face. "I would venture to say that almost everyone in America lost someone close to them from the plague."

Seeing the pain in the doctor's face, Paige began to feel that she and the doctor had more in common than she had at first thought. Perhaps she had at least a chance of getting some answers. Whether it was her imagination or not, she was going to push forward. "Dr. Parks, I would guess that you have been just as devastated as myself, as well as countless others. Would it be safe to say that you personally have done everything within your power to find some answers yourself?"

The smile that made Lauren Parks appear so beautiful vanished and was replaced by a much darker expression. Paige had seen that expression countless times staring back at her from a mirror. For Paige, it was a combination of many emotions-- anger, depression, hopelessness, and an overall sense of fatality.

"Ms. Summers, I'm not at liberty to share with you any of my research projects, but I will tell you what I can, and possibly give you a direction that with tenacity will lead you to some partial conclusions."

If nothing else, Paige felt that at least she had a start. She didn't know where this was going to lead her, but it didn't matter, not as long as her path led to the truth. She pulled out the digital voice recorder that she used for all of her interviews. As soon as she placed it on the desk, Dr.Parks shook her head "no" and reached over turning the recorder off and put it in her desk drawer.

"I'll give it back once the interview is finished, but for today you are going to have to take notes."

Finding the doctor did not want to be recorded confused Paige at first, but she reached into her laptop bag to get out her Mac to take notes on.

Understanding the unasked question, Dr. Parks explained, "This interview never happened. What I'm about to tell you is from one of your many anonymous sources. If you can agree to that, then we can continue." She said it so plainly in such a "matter of fact" manner, Paige thought that this lady had given these types of interviews before or at least she had put some thought into this one well before Paige arrived.

"I understand and agree. I will not use your name, your position, or any reference that could be linked to you. We are used to protecting the identity of our sources at the magazine. Do you mind if I use my laptop to take notes?"

Dr. Parks agreed and they began the interview. "I'll start by letting you know that there has never been something of this magnitude happen anywhere in the world. Nothing even close to this has ever been recorded. This plague hit and in one day killed millions. There are many things that have left us in the dark. The timing of the whole thing terrifies me."

Page looked at the doctor quizzically. "I don't understand what you mean when you say the timing of the plague."

Dr. Parks went over to the coffee pot that was set up next to her desk and began to pour herself a cup. "Would you like some coffee?"

"No, thank you," Page answered still waiting to hear the doctor's answer to her question.

Dr. Parks finished pouring a cup of coffee, returned to her desk, and sat down. She took a sip and began to talk. "When I say timing, it's because I have no other word to explain the way this happened. You see, for people to die of a plague, they have to first contract the disease. Although many of the people who died were close to someone else who died, there is no physical way a disease can spread across the globe without being stopped somewhere. Except this one did. Another thing that surprisingly isn't being talked about more is that as far as we can tell, all of the people died at approximately the same time across the globe. That just can't happen. The best guess so far is that it was some sort of military experiment that went haywire.

Here at the Center, we are still in the process of researching the plague using first-hand knowledge gathered from thousands of victims' families and friends. We also are linked with several other research centers across the U.S. doing the same thing."

All combined it was the largest project any of them had been connected to. As a nationwide group, they were researching tens of millions of victims. The results so far had only yielded more questions. In the U.S. alone the total count of victims was around one hundred fifty million. According to the sheer numbers, the effects of this plague had not even been felt yet. According to the doctor, no known link connected the victims. Some of the victims may have had serious conditions, but others had nothing that could be found.

"One thing that is baffling is that as far as we can tell, no one under the age of five has been left alive."

Page was very surprised to hear that. "What does that mean?" she asked.

"Quite frankly, it means that I'm more than a little nervous. I need to find some evidence that we can reproduce. When I say we, I'm talking about the human race." She then looked directly at Page with an expression that left no room for doubt that she was serious. "As you are reaching out to your contacts in the news world, have them look for pregnancies in other countries as well. I think you will find that there are no pregnant women to be found... anywhere."

Paige finished typing her notes and when the interview came to an end, she thanked the doctor for her time. Dr. Parks handed the digital voice recorder back to Paige and walked her back to the main entrance. She said before Paige had a chance to thank her. "I'm sorry I couldn't have been any help to you. Better luck with your next interview."

Paige could see that the young man at the receptionist desk was paying attention. "I understand. Thanks for your time, Doctor."

"She wanted a detailed list of all our contributors," she heard the doctor tell the young man as the electronic doors closed behind her. It was obvious she was trying to keep him from being overly curious.

Paige barely made it to her car before she got hit with a wave of nausea springing from what she had just learned. The implications of what she had heard were more devastating than anything she could imagine. Paige was beginning to understand why she had heard nothing from the scientific community and why Dr. Parks refused to go on record. If this information came from official channels, it could cause widespread panic even worse than what was already happening. She had heard about nice neighborhoods that were now becoming war zones for different gangs. People all around the country were living in fear. She wondered what it was like in other countries if it was this bad in the U.S.

Sitting in her car parked in the parking lot trying to calm her sick stomach, she knew she still had a lot of work to do. She started her car and headed to her office. She had a huge job in front of her, and it would have to start at her desk getting things organized.

Once at the magazine complex, Paige went straight to her office. There was a large neon sign on the front lawn of the complex that showed a cityscape with the words "Around Town" written around the city. It had turned out to be a catchy logo.

Being a columnist for Around Town afforded Paige her own private office, which today she was glad she had. She was able to go in and shut the door for privacy, a habit she had developed whenever she was working on a story. Paige started pacing back and forth in front of her desk. She knew the only way to get anything done was to calm down and organize her thoughts, but that was extremely difficult with her mind and emotions working towards a breaking point. Finally, she sat down and pulled out her Mac, turned it on, and opened the notes she had taken during her talk with Dr. Parks. She opened a second blank document to start writing down her own thoughts. She saved it, naming it "The Plague." She planned to use this file to keep everything together in one place that she could find that would relate to what had happened. Over what she hoped would be a short period of time, she would combine and condense all this information into a column for the magazine.

Over the next few hours, she started calling doctors' offices, specifically obstetricians, in the hopes of proving Dr. Parks wrong, but her first few hours proved to be no help. Over the next two days, she decided to broaden her search to other parts of the country. Paige called obstetricians from Miami to Las Angeles. When she found that none had any pregnant women as patients, she then tried New York and Chicago.

After two days of searching and talking to hundreds of doctors, Paige decided to call one more doctor. She called the Center for Medical Research. She didn't introduce herself, but instead just asked for Dr. Parks. When the doctor came on the line, Paige went straight to her question. "Dr. Parks, this is Paige Summers. We talked a few days ago. In your opinion, how long do we have left?"

"If you really want to hear my opinion, we could meet for coffee in about an hour," Dr. Parks said.

Paige agreed, and the two of them decided on a coffee shop Paige was familiar with. This time, she made it a point to leave her digital recorder in her office as she left.

Paige got to the coffee shop before Dr. Parks, sat down at a booth, and ordered a mocha latte. Dr. Parks arrived before the latte did and gave the waitress her order. It didn't take them long to get right to the reason for their meeting. Dr. Parks was the first to get started on the topic. "I assume that since our first meeting that you have done some research yourself," she said.

"Yes, I have, Dr. Parks, and so far, I don't see a light at the end of the tunnel. It seems that whatever this plague was, it has affected everyone. Are you telling me that the world as we know it will cease to exist?"

Dr. Parks looked at her unblinkingly. "I'm not saying that it will 'cease to exist.' I'm saying that our world ended on the day of the plague. This is the end of the human race. Not only that, but it's going to get more and more difficult as time moves forward. There will come a point where those who died in the plague will be considered the lucky ones."

Feeling sick with dread, she slid the latte away from her. Even the smell of it was making her nauseous. She hadn't known what to expect from this talk with Dr. Parks, but her answer was taking her in a direction that she wasn't ready to accept. "Are you alone in this belief or are there other researchers who share your … diagnosis?"

The expression on the doctor's face softened. "This is the conclusion that is being reached across the globe. We have all agreed not to talk about this publicly because it would cause a panic, the likes of which has never been seen."

"Then why have you told me?"

"I really don't know. I've asked myself that same question several times since our first meeting, and I come up with different answers all the time. Ms. Summers, I don't want to start a panic, but at the same time, I don't think I have the right to keep this a secret. I believe it's going to be worse here in the U.S. than in some other parts of the world."

Now Paige was really confused. She didn't understand how things could be worse for the U.S. "What makes you say that?"

The Dr. asked for her email address and promised to send her some articles on interdependence. "As a culture, we have each become dependent on each other for different parts of our survival. This gives people the ability to focus on what they do best. For example, you may be great at growing things while I can make cars. People in general depend on farmers and ranchers to grow food, while farmers and ranchers need the equipment that other people can build. Even though this is a good thing for society, it can also be very dangerous under some circumstances. On the night of the plague, the U.S. lost millions upon millions of people, and that has created a devastating effect that has not been fully felt yet. Our recent loss alone has been crippling, but even worse will be the loss of future generations. If a person your age gets to the point where you can no longer keep up with the physical labor it takes for you to survive, there will no longer be a younger generation to step into a position to help."

Dr. Parks summed up her point. "Once people from our generation get too old to work on a farm, how are we going to eat?" She let that soak in before going on. "And in countries like the U.S., that question gets a lot more intricate, and frankly a lot more terrifying. It's bad enough to think that we may be the last generation on earth. It's a whole lot worse to realize how pitiful our last few years are going to be. I'm truly afraid of what my life will be like twenty years from now."

By the end of the conversation, Paige felt even worse than she did before meeting with the doctor. However, the professional in her kept telling her that no matter how she felt, she had a lot of work to get done. Paige felt in her gut that this woman was no crackpot. The small amount of research she had done herself confirmed what the doctor had told her. She also knew her editor was going to fight her on this story and that the magazine may choose not to print the story. Despite all of that, Paige knew it had to be written, damn the torpedos, full speed ahead. She went back to her office and started to work.

Chapter Four

MARCO Corsetti had been the Prime Minister of Italy for the last two years. Even though the last few months had been a nightmare, Marco saw some opportunity in the way things were happening.

All the leaders of the European Union had agreed to meet together to discuss what their options were for working together to handle this global crisis, which is what it was. This plague had touched every community of every nation on the planet. The European Union was in a desperate situation.

Corsetti saw all of this as an open invitation. In the meeting, Marco put forward the idea of all of their countries coming together to form one nation, a united front that would benefit them all equally. The idea was initially laughed at by some of the traditionally more wealthy countries, but they almost instantly realized that their countries had been hit just as hard or harder than the much poorer nations. In reality it was a proposal, that by all rights, should have been laughed at by everyone. It was truly unreal how one by one everyone there agreed that all of their countries were in a dire position and joining together under one unified governmental system may be their best hope for survival.

Marco had expected a lot more resistance than he got. He came to the meeting with several persuasive arguments to support his proposal. He was shocked at how easily and quickly the proposal was accepted.

So in just a few weeks, the European Union dissolved, and out of the ashes was born the New World Order.

Marco Corsetti was named Prime Minister of the New World Order, so at the stroke of a pen, twenty-eight nations became one and Marco Corsetti was now one of the most powerful and influential people on Earth.

One of the first challenges Corsetti had was creating a system that would cement these nations to each other in a way that would prove almost impossible to dissolve. He pulled together a council made up of people who specialized in a wide variety of fields. Among the group were political experts, scientists, engineers, economists, marketing gurus, computer programmers, and military leaders from each nation. They were all brought together to create a system that would completely lock the citizens of these nations together. The system also had to have the flexibility to be able to bring other nations into it quickly.

After only a month his think tank came up with a system they believed would work. They believed their idea would unify the people in these countries so completely that it would be virtually impossible to reverse.

The idea was to set up an electronic credit system that would replace, and then eliminate, the currencies of all the nations in the system. The system they designed would make day-to-day life much easier for the citizens.

Each person would have a microchip injected into them that would attach itself to the person's nervous system. The chip they designed was truly the most innovative and ambitious device ever imagined. The list of benefits it provided was large and it could add even more as they were made available. The chip itself was so small it could be injected, and it was powered by the human body, so as long as the host was alive, the chip would stay powered.

It could send and receive information using a Bluetooth antenna approximately the diameter of a human hair. The wrist and forehead were the two best places for the antenna to be located for the signal to interact with both the chip and the integrated system of the central government.

Once a person was loaded into the system, they could no longer have their identity stolen, they could travel and work in any of the countries that were aligned with the system. There would be no need for a passport, driver's license, or any other kind of identification. Their bank account would also be part of the system so they would no longer have to carry any kind of currency on their person. They would be able to pay for anything and get paid by anyone with no effort from either party.

There would, of course, be a short period of transition where both the current state of trade and the proposed system would exist simultaneously.

The quicker they could accomplish the transition, the better it would be for everyone concerned, and once it was completed, almost every aspect of a person's life would be tied to the system.

The possibilities for this new system were truly amazing. It could coordinate globally and have billions of users simultaneously. This would revolutionize commerce on the entire globe. It could also interact with the existing communication networks across the globe, so the infrastructure was already in place. That would make the implementation of the system very fast as well as pain-free. The New World Order could have this system implemented across all of the former countries and fully operational in a matter of months.

Liking what he saw, Minister Corsetti gave the order to put the system into operation.

One of his first political moves as Prime Minister of The New World Order would be to establish allies with the nations of the rest of the world. He had almost immediately received congratulatory statements from several of the world leaders, including the President of the United States, the Russian Prime Minister, and the Israeli Prime Minister. He intended to draw up treaties with each of them as well as trade agreements.

Corsetti faced a small amount of disagreement from a few of his cabinet members. Most of the disagreement was because he had made overtures on entering into a treaty and trade agreement with Israel. The arguments came because of Israel's religious stance. He held firm in the face of his opposition because he believed that a good relationship with Israel was key to getting a secure link to the United States.

Even though the U.S.A. was hit harder by the plague than many other countries, it was still one of the main economic forces on the globe. Even if the U.S. weren't a factor in all of this, he still saw Israel as a juicy morsel that was ripe for the picking. The plan was set into motion when the Israeli prime minister, Ephraim Bar Aaron, accepted his invitation for a meeting in Rome.

The weather forecast was for a beautiful day, so Corsetti made the decision to have the Colosseum closed for that day so they could have the meeting there. He was at a conference table with his advisers and aids when he made the announcement.

"Sir," one of his aides decided to speak up. "The Israeli prime minister will likely be offended by that choice of venue because of how many Jews were killed in the Colosseum."

Corsetti took a sip of his spiced wine called Conditum Paradoxum, savored the taste, and then said to the group as a whole, "I'm going to use the history of the Colosseum to our advantage. We will use this to mark the new beginning of our relationship with Israel. Where it once was a symbol of dread, it will now be a symbol of hope and peace. If you study your history of the Roman games, you will find that it was Jewish slaves who built the arena, but it was the Christians who were most often sent there to die. That didn't become a notable event until Nero became Emperor."

No one at the table said anything in response. Corsetti took another sip of his wine and allowed the silence to linger long enough for the people sitting around the table to become a little uncomfortable, then he broke the silence. "I'm going to use this meeting to offer our aid in rebuilding their temple."

He paused again seeing the shock on some faces and confusion on others. "This will establish us as the main benefactor of Israel. We will be seen as their most ardent supporter. That type of symbolic recognition will become incredibly valuable, and it will be the stepping-stone that will help us to become the most powerful government on the planet. Not even the vaunted United States will be able to compare to our New World Order."

CHAPTER FIVE

E VEN though the plague was a worldwide event, every individual community was focused on local recovery efforts. Every business was
struck by the waves of the plague, some worse than others. The company
Mike worked for, Life Express, lost people from every shift and as a result,
they were scrambling to replace their lost employees. They still maintained
the same number of crews, but each crew was down to just two teams
instead of the three or four that they normally ran. Mike slipped into a
routine that allowed him to get through his shift with very little interaction
with his coworkers. The people who worked on his shift all knew someone
who had died in the plague but none of them had lost someone as close as a
wife or daughter. Most of them were relieved when they realized that Mike
wanted to be left alone. Everyone was dealing with this tragedy in the best
way they could.

One other person on the team who seemed to want to be alone was
Alter Cagan. He always had his laptop at the station and if he wasn't on a
run, he spent his time in the break room entranced with something on the
computer.

One day, they were all in the break room. Alter was at a table en-
grossed with whatever it was on his laptop that had his undivided attention,
and Mike was sitting off to the side not really paying attention to anyone.
The two girls were watching a special report about the dissolving of European Union.

"Hey, Alter and Mike, ya'll should listen to this. It sounds like the E.U.
is breaking apart," Donna said over her shoulder.

Mike and Alter missed the beginning of the show, but even so, it was fairly easy to catch up with what was being said. The announcer reported that the European Union was officially dissolved and most of the countries that had been part of the Union had now come together to form one nation named "The New World Order". This new nation had a central government with one man heading that government. The leader, a man by the name of Marco Corsetti, had announced meetings with leaders of other nations to discuss trade agreements. Corsetti had meetings scheduled with China, Russia, and Israel, with other announcements coming soon.

When the news story ended everyone in the room just sat there without saying a word. The world seemed to be changing at a rate that none of them could quite grasp.

Then finally, it was Alter who broke the silence. "That's likely the first of many changes we are going to see."

No one seemed to understand what he possibly meant and the conversation slowly faded away until the first call came in. From the first call until the end of the shift the action was nonstop, so there wasn't any more conversation about anything other than the call that each team was on at the moment.

Mike was teamed up with Donna, and between calls she commented that she wondered what Alter had been so caught up in with his computer.

Mike answered, "I don't care, as long as he does his job, it doesn't affect me."

Even before the plague hit and Mike had been changed by his personal loss, he had no patience for idle gossip, and that was the direction this conversation seemed to be going. At the end of the shift, he did make it a point to say something to Alter. As they were walking out to their cars, he called Alter aside. "Just to let you know, I think you do a great job, so what I'm about to say has nothing to do with the way you do your job. I figured I would let you know that some people are overly curious about whatever it is you are doing on your computer between calls. Quite frankly, as long as you do your job the way you do, I don't think it's anybody's business. I just thought you should know, that's all."

Alter had a halfhearted smile, slightly shook his head, and said, "I lost a very good friend to the plague, and I've been studying some research he had been doing to see if I can find some answers."

That was the one thing Alter could say that Mike could completely empathize with. He also wanted answers but was at a total loss on how to go about finding them. "Alter, I hope you find some answers," he said.

"Actually, I have. If you're not doing anything else, I could come by and share some information with you."

That was definitely not what Mike expected and even though he had no desire to spend his time with people, something about Alter's manner made him curious. He agreed, and both of them headed over to Mike's house.

Once they got to his house Mike offered to make some coffee for both of them. Alter thanked him and then asked if he could set his laptop up on the dining room table.

"Sure, go ahead," Mike said as he walked to the counter to the coffee machine. It was one of those units that will brew one cup at a time very quickly. He got the first cup brewed and switched the coffee pod for a second. "What do you take in yours?"

"Black is fine," Alter answered while looking at the laptop.

Once the two of them were sitting at the table each with a cup of coffee, Alter pushed the laptop a little off to the side and began to tell Mike the story of his childhood friend, Ben Cotler.

Alter was born in Israel. Surprisingly, his family was one of the few families in Israel who lived devout lives according to the Hebrew religion. By the time Alter was twelve years old his father accepted a job offer and moved his family to America. They were surprised and pleased to find out that the Jewish community was easy to find and get grafted into. After only a year in the U.S., they bought a house in a predominately Jewish neighborhood located in Atlanta, Georgia. Several families from the community made it a point to welcome their new neighbors and one of those families was the Cotler family. Like the Cagans, they held strongly to their Jewish faith. They also had a son around the same age as Alter. His name was Ben. It didn't take long for the two boys to become good friends. They stayed close friends through high school. Alter was a year older than Ben, so he graduated and headed to college a year earlier than Ben.

It was in that first year of college that Alter received a very long letter from his friend. In the letter, Ben explained that when he got home, he was going to get some news that may be difficult, so he wanted to explain his side of things. In the letter, Ben explained that he had converted to

Christianity, and as a result, his family had given him the ultimatum of either denouncing Christianity or he would be disowned.

Much to Alter's amusement, it was a girl that started all of this. Ben had started dating this girl even before Alter had left for college, and Alter had agreed to keep their relationship to himself.

When he got home for the summer, things had gotten progressively worse. Ben's parents had blamed Alter of being part of a conspiracy to drive a wedge between them and their son. The whole situation had turned into some kind of family feud. Even through all of that, Alter and Ben remained the best of friends, but they kept their friendship a secret from both sets of parents.

To make matters worse, Ben and Megan, the girl he had been dating, got married. Alter had quietly attended the wedding, all the time wondering how much commitment Ben had.

Ben received several scholarships and much to Alter's surprise, he went to a Christian university with his major in theology. He told Alter that he was going to be a minister.

It turned out that Ben was serious about becoming a minister. Over the next few years, Alter kept in touch with Ben and Megan. Ben sent him loads of research on why he believed that Jesus was and is the Messiah the Jews were waiting for. Alter thought it was interesting and even skimmed through bits and pieces of the files Ben had sent him.

Then a couple of months before the plague hit, Ben showed up at Alter's door out of the blue. He told Alter that he had been given a burden to pray for him to accept the Messiah, and that burden had been getting stronger by the day. The two of them talked for a long time, and Alter would have been lying if he said that he felt no pull to believe what his friend was telling him. In the end, though, he didn't fully believe what Ben was telling him. They agreed to meet again later and discuss the matter, but later never came.

Ben and his wife Megan were victims of the plague.

Alter didn't find out that they had died until a few days after the plague, when he had gone by to check on them. When he found no one at the house, it only took a quick inquiry at the morgue to find out they were among those who had passed away. Then, thinking of their last conversation he went to the police department to get permission to go through Ben's research to see if his friend had left him any information on his newfound beliefs. The police department agreed to let him look as long as an officer went with him. They explained that it had become difficult to keep out loot-ers and vandals and a police presence would probably be a good thing while Alter was there. Alter readily agreed and scheduled a day to meet the officer at the house.

Alter explained to Mike that what he had been studying on his laptop at work were the research files that he had found on Ben's computer.

Even though Mike thought the story was interesting, he didn't under-stand why Alter was telling him all this. He took a sip of his coffee, set the cup down, and asked, "I'm not sure what it is you are trying to tell me."

"It's about a connection that I think I've found between Ben's research and the plague. The reason I'm talking to you is because you have been affected more profoundly than anyone I know. Something tells me that you should hear the things I'm learning. I don't have a reason why--it's just a gut feeling."

Now Mike was definitely curious. When he first lost Eve and Amy, he was desperate for answers but there were none to be found. Over the last few weeks, his mental state had switched from desperation to chronic depression.

Alter plugged a thumb drive into his laptop. Mike thought he was opening something up in the drive but then after about a minute of saying nothing, he pulled the thumb drive out and handed it to Mike.

"There's a lot of information on here and it will take you some time to go through it all. The file called 'conclusions' is what I have come up with. If you decide to go through all of this, I would like to hear your thoughts when you are done."

Mike accepted the drive and said he would get on it right away. Alter seemed pleased and said he should head home. He stopped at the door and with a serious expression on his face, he asked Mike not to share this infor-mation with anyone. Mike thought that was a strange request but agreed not to let anyone know about whatever this information was.

Later that evening he plugged the thumb drive into his laptop and opened it up. The information was divided up into individual files. The first was named "Yeshua is Messiah". The last simply said "Conclusion". His nor-mal impulse would be to start with that last file, but for reasons he couldn't name, he started with the first file.

Ben-Elohim, the son of God, the Messiah, is the savior of the world. That was the first sentence of the file. It went on to explain that there were over three hundred prophecies in the Tanakh, which Mike later learned was where the Old Testament writings came from, where all of the prophecies had been perfectly fulfilled by Yeshua or Jesus. It went on to say that scientifically and mathematically that was impossible. According to mathematician Peter Stoner, the probabilities of any one person fulfilling even 48 of the over 324 Messianic prophecies found in the Tanakh would be 1 in 10^{157}* (*1 followed by 157 zeros). Yet all 324 prophecies were fulfilled. Even for Mike, that was amazing. He couldn't help but think his wife Julie would have loved to be able to read this.

Over the next two days, he found himself going back to the files Alter had put on his laptop. They had three days off before the evening shift started, so he asked Alter to come by during their break so he could ask a few questions.

That next morning Alter showed up at Mike's house. Mike invited him in and asked if he had eaten breakfast yet.

"I have, thank you, but I could definitely go for another cup of coffee."

So once again Mike made a couple cups of coffee and the two of them sat down at the table.

"You went through that material a lot quicker than I expected you to," Alter said after taking his first sip of coffee.

"Well, that's why I asked you to come over. I haven't gone through all of it yet, and as interesting as it is, I don't see any relevance there to what happened to us. So, I'm not sure why you wanted me to read all this."

Alter put his cup down on the table slowly, then closed his eyes and bowed his head down slightly. After a few seconds, he looked up at Mike with a somber expression. "Okay, but please promise me that you will finish reading the files. Most of the information is from Ben and he was much better at explaining things than I am."

Mike could see that Alter was extremely serious about whatever it was they were about to talk about, so he assured Alter that he would finish reading the files. He could see the relief written all over Alter's face. Then with no further hesitation Alter began. "There are several passages in the New Testament that mention the gathering together of the children of God. Most of the modern church called it the rapture of the church. My theory is that just like we Jews were wrong about who the Messiah was, the church was wrong about how the rapture would happen."

Suddenly Mike could see where Alter was going with this and he didn't like it. "Are you trying to tell me that this plague was God rapturing his church?" he asked with a look of incredulity on his face.

For his part, Alter seemed to expect this kind of reaction. "I am, but let me explain my reasons before you blow up." He paused and then continued.

"When Jesus was talking to Nicodemus, he said that unless you are born again you cannot see the Kingdom of God. Then Nicodemus asked how could a man go back into his mother's womb and be born again. Nicodemus was taking what he said literally, but Jesus was talking about a man's spirit being made new. First Corinthians chapter fifteen verse fifty tells us that our physical bodies cannot inherit the Kingdom of God. Then it says a few verses later that our dying bodies will be transformed into bodies that will never die. Who's to say that when that transformation happens, our physical body, which is just a shell, won't be discarded and left here on earth. To everyone who was not taken, it would look like a horrible worldwide plague."

Everything within him made Mike want to lash out against what Alter was saying, but something made him stop and consider what was being suggested. "There's a flaw in your theory," Mike said and went on. "The flaw is, I'm a Christian and I'm sitting here talking to you. So why am I here?"

Alter knew this part of the conversation was coming, but knowing didn't help him prepare for it. Mike was a good man and Alter didn't want to insult him in any way. At the same time, he could see no easy way around this. Nevertheless, he spoke slowly trying to choose his words carefully. "You believe that Jesus is the son of God and that God raised him from the dead, right?"

"Of course, I do," Mike answered.

"Well, not to sound judgmental, but do you call yourself a Christian because you don't have any other group that you want to line yourself up with, or because Yeshua is truly your Lord? The reason I ask it like that is that Americans don't really have a reference we can use to fully understand the concept of Lord. In his letter to the church in Rome, the Apostle Paul said in chapter ten verse nine says that if you declare with your mouth the Lord Jesus Christ and believe in your heart that God raised him from the dead, you will be saved. In Jewish culture, there is an innate understanding of what it means to declare someone as Lord. Unfortunately, here in America, it's just words without real meaning. If someone is your Lord, then you no longer have any personal rights. You are now that person's property."

For his part, Mike had never considered a conversation like this one. His mind suddenly went to Julie and Sarah and how they looked when he found them. They were both in a relaxed position, and it looked like they may have been watching T.V. when it happened. There had been a movie on the DVD player, and there was no way to tell, but it could have been around the same time that the first call had come in that night.

Then Alter's voice brought him back to the moment. "Obviously, I'm in no position to say why you are still here, because up until recently I didn't even believe that the Messiah had come, so to tell you the truth, this is all new to me."

"But now you do believe that Jesus was the Messiah?" Mike asked.

"I know that Yeshua is the Messiah, not that he was the Messiah."

Talking with Alter like this forced Mike to take a look at himself, and when he did, he didn't exactly like what he saw. He was a man of morals who even believed in putting the needs of others before his own. Even so, a Bible verse came to mind from out of nowhere. He couldn't find the specific verse to save his life, but he did know that it was somewhere in the New Testament. He could only just remember a paraphrase of the verse that he heard a preacher say. It went something like, "So you believe, do you? Good for you, the demons in hell believe too." His focus throughout his life was on being a good husband and good father, and all his memories told him that he had succeeded in that. Even so, sitting here talking to Alter, he couldn't help but wonder if he had missed out on something even more important.

He remembered the change in Sarah and then later in Julie. It had started after Sarah had moved out to live on her own. She met this guy at school and started attending church with him. After a while, she called and asked Mike and Julie to come to visit her church. Since it was Sarah who asked, they accepted at once. All in all, it was a very enjoyable experience for them both. The people at the church were friendly and welcoming without being pushy, and the preacher actually seemed like a real guy, and not someone who was all show.

Sarah mentioned that a small group of people was going to meet at her house that evening to hang out and get to know each other and asked if they would like to join them. Since they never missed a chance to spend time with their baby girl, they immediately said that they would be there. From that time forward they had started attending regularly. Even though Mike truly enjoyed being with the people of the church, Julie took it to another level. She started studying as if she were getting ready for a final exam in college. Then one Sunday morning when the preacher gave the altar call, Julie went forward to be prayed for.

Mike had to admit that after this, there was a marked difference in his wife, and he also would have to admit that he liked the change. He couldn't say how, but their relationship changed as well. It was not overnight, but over a few months it had gotten better. Which for him was hard to believe, because as far as he was concerned it was already perfect.

Mike remembered that he had been happy that Julie had found a deeper meaning, but he had been raised in the church and didn't believe he needed to make any more of a commitment than he already had. Thinking back on it, Mike couldn't help but wonder if he had made an incredible mistake.

Since the day of the plague, he never returned to the church they had attended together, mainly because he just didn't want to bring up painful memories. Now, talking to Alter, he decided that he would drop by there tomorrow, if for no other reason than to put a stop to all these nagging doubts he felt.

CHAPTER SIX

O N Tuesday morning, the talk with Alter from the day before was still going through Mike's head. He had decided that after some breakfast he would drive over to the church and put his doubts to rest. The church always had staff members there during the day even if there were no services, so he felt sure there would be someone there even if it was a Tuesday.

When he pulled into the parking lot, the church bus was sitting where it was typically parked, but there were no other cars in the parking lot. He parked his car and walked towards one of the outside doors. He used a side entrance that he knew was the closest entry to the church office.

There were several notices taped to the door from the power and water companies, late bills, and a notice of cancellation. Mike didn't need to look further but he couldn't help himself.

This particular church had a parsonage on the property, a home that the congregation supplied for the Senior Pastor, so Mike decided to walk over there. There was the same type of notices at the home. There was one additional note taped to the door saying where the car had been towed. He decided to go through his contact list to see if he had any numbers from some of the others that were at the church. He did find a couple of numbers. One was disconnected, and there was no answer on the other. He hung up as the voice mail started. That at least was hopeful. The disconnected number likely belonged to someone who had died in the plague, but the one with no answer gave him some hope.

On his way back to the car, his phone rang and the name on the caller I.D. was Matthew Hayes, the number no one had answered. He answered it immediately. "Hello?"

"Hi, this is Debbie Hayes, did you just call this number?"

"Hi, yes, this is Mike Daniels, and I was trying to reach your husband, Matthew."

There was a slight pause before she answered, "Oh, yes, I remember. Didn't you and your wife go to the same church with Matt?"

At this point, Mike was feeling a bit silly, and he didn't know exactly where to go from here. Before he could answer her question, though, Matt's wife continued. "Well, I'm sorry to tell you this, but Matt was taken by the plague, just like so many others. I just never had his phone turned off. I'll even call it from time to time just to hear his voice. It sounds like he's right there on the line with me."

"I'm so sorry to hear about your loss." Mike explained that it had been a while since he had been to the church and was just trying to get reconnected with some of the people there. Mrs. Hayes gave him a couple of names that he could try to reach.

"I don't have their numbers, but I'm sure you should be able to find them. I'm sorry that I'm not much help for you."

When the conversation ended, Mike drove on with a heavy sense of doom hanging over him like a thick fog, so thick you could feel the darkness.

Mike stopped at a grocery store to pick up some things before going home. As he walked through the aisle one of the magazines caught his eye.

"Are we the Last Generation on Earth?"

He picked up the news magazine and that was the title of the article that was advertised on the cover. Since his life had been what it was over the last few months, he bought the magazine and took it home to read it.

From the day the plague had hit, Mike had just been going on autopilot without even wanting to pay attention to what was happening to those around him. Mike had a definite feeling that he was isolated from the rest of the world. His recent talk with Alter hadn't helped that feeling, but he did at least have a direction to go towards.

He didn't pick up the magazine until later that evening. He had gotten into the routine of coming home and eating his diner, which was normally no more than what could barely be called a sandwich. Just two pieces of bread with a couple of slices of roast beef and some cheese. He didn't even bother to put any mayo or mustard on it. He would grab a coke out of the fridge if there were any or just a glass of water. Then he would eat the sandwich in the living room sitting in a recliner. He still couldn't bring himself to sit on the couch. That's where Julie had been when he found her and

Sarah. Some nights he would turn the TV on and some he wouldn't. Even with the TV on, he never actually watched what was on. It was just white noise. Without Julie or Sarah, there was no reason to put forth any effort to go on with life. What if they hadn't died? What if they were called home to Jesus and left their old bodies behind for new ones? The thought didn't ease his pain of loss, but it did give him a vague sense of hope.

"Lord, please forgive me for missing what has been right in front of my eyes all of my life. I don't know if this means that I'm lost forever or if there is still a chance for me. If there is a chance, Lord, please accept me as a new believer in you."

It was a simple prayer, but it came from his heart and Mike knew that it was the first time he had ever prayed from his heart. For the first time he noticed that he had been crying. His face was wet with tears, and he felt as if a huge weight that had been sitting on his chest had been removed.

Mike got up, went to the sink, washed his face, and dried it. Then out of the corner of his eye, he saw the magazine that he had picked up earlier.

The title of the article got his attention. It was written by a local columnist, Paige somebody. He thought he remembered the name from some of the articles Julie had read. He started reading the article.

As troubling as it is to read, let me assure you, it's certainly harder to write. But I don't have a choice. I have to get this story out...

The plague that rocked our planet months ago is not dead yet. Tendrils of its menacing grasp still reach out and touch every one of us. And the most disturbing part is that we don't even know it's happening.

Many aspects of the plague have gone unreported, undocumented. In the next couple of paragraphs, I'm going to tell you what no one has told you yet.

Like many of you, I am one of the surviving victims of the plague. I lost my niece and shortly after, my best friend in the entire world--my sister. Their loss wrecked me. Their loss has plagued my mind more than the inestimable sickness that has plagued our planet.

It's affected us all on a very personal level. If you combine all the deaths in both world wars, they would only be a small fraction of the number of people we lost in just...one...day. One billion people and counting.

That's only a mathematical guess based on the reported deaths. Some countries are not providing any official numbers, but several statisticians agree that a billion people is a conservative enough number.

Saying that the number of deaths is conservative feels cheap, as if what we lost could be made up or accounted for later. But what we've lost is never coming back and can never be replaced. Devastating would be a truer representation of what that number means.

We've been left wiped out mentally and emotionally. Resources and finances have been catastrophically hit, leaving a crater as large as the ocean. Still, we have no answers.

Looking at the best-case scenario, it would take a few generations for us to recover. But this is not the best case. It's one of the worst.

From what I've been able to gather, no one under the age of five survived the plague. And those few under the age of fifteen are barely sustaining themselves. What does that mean? Our youngest generation is gone.

My niece was only five years old. Her life was just beginning when the plague took her. Her mother, my sister, couldn't live in a world where Rosalie was not. She ended her life in the aftershock of the plague, and I lost everything I've ever held dear.

I lost my hope and will to survive. I shut myself in, drowned out my nightmares, and medicated my sorrow. This is the state I see the rest of the world in; hopeless, crying for its lost baby, broken beyond repair.

We lost all our children, and because of that, the suicide rate of women and mothers all over the globe has skyrocketed. Miscarriages and stillborn babies littered hospitals and morgues.

My research has spanned the entire U.S., and I have not found a single pregnant woman. I am willing to bet that it's the same in every other country.

The plague infected all of us, and it lives in everybody that still breathes and moves, but we don't even have a name for it, or worse--a cure.

Most of the doctors I've interviewed told me that my conclusions are way off. They tried to dissuade me with medical jargon and words that were far beyond my schooling or comprehension. My psychology professor once said that it's a common habit of highly educated people--to use terminology that is difficult to understand when they don't know what they are talking about, and they don't want to admit that to you. But I think it was more than the fact that they didn't want me to understand. It was that they didn't understand, and no one has ever been held accountable for what they are saying.

They aren't any closer to knowing what ravaged our planet and why. And they're scared. They're scared because now...we face extinction.

A few scientists, who wish to remain anonymous, agree with me. According to their calculations, our race will not last beyond the current generation.

What's worse is human beings are interdependent. We rely, like a colony of ants, on each other. And our anthill just took a flattening blow.

That plague is known as an extinction event, but this is not like any you've seen in the movies. An asteroid isn't heading towards earth, barreling through our atmosphere. The "asteroid" has already hit, and we are dead.

Unless we can come up with a way to mass reproduce and repopulate our dying earth, the human race is over.

I don't expect you to read this article and accept what I am saying, but I do expect you to go in search of your own answers like I have. And hopefully, you'll prove me wrong.

I invite all of you to respond to me, challenge me on this!

His next shift started tomorrow. He put the magazine in his "go bag" for work. He was going to take this and show it to Alter. After the talk that they had when Alter had paid him a visit here at his house, he was curious about what Alter's take on this would be. This was also a local magazine, so he thought he would pay this girl "Paige Summers" a visit and see if she had any more information that she had not put in the article. He would have plenty of time in the mornings because he was starting second shift, which ran from three in the afternoon to eleven at night.

CHAPTER SEVEN

T HE paper tore under the weight of her pen, dragging an obscure, black line through two more pages of the notebook.

"Dammit," she said under her breath.

If someone had asked her at the wrong moment how long it had been since the plague, Paige couldn't have imagined an answer. It felt like this had been her entire life, but also that it had just happened a few moments ago. It was hard to believe that less than a year ago the only thing that created tension was an approaching deadline for a story she was writing. She still had deadlines to meet, but they no longer seemed to have world-shattering importance the way they used to.

Now her frustration came from something different, and the problem was, she couldn't pinpoint what exactly caused her so much frustration. The easy explanation was for her to just say that it was the plague. Sometimes she told herself that. Deep in her subconscious, she knew something was nagging at her just beneath the surface.

Her editor had been visibly disturbed by her story, but he told her to go ahead with it. When she thought about what she had discovered, Paige felt torn between giving up and doing anything she could to stop this insanity.

Paige had had a special relationship with her twin sister Amanda. Their mother told them a story about the night they were born. She said they had been born on a Halloween night just shy of midnight, and when the nurses tried to separate them, they shrieked like banshees until they were put back together again. Growing up, they were more than just twins--they were more like two halves of the same person. They both liked the same ice cream flavors, music, shows on T.V., and on and on. They even knew what each other thought. People thought that they were bonded together for life, until one day when a guy came into the picture.

It happened in college and his name was Thomas Ridgefield. He was charming and handsome, dedicated to his academic career--everything a girl would want out of a boyfriend. But there was something different about him. Something was off in the way he acted, like there was something else under the surface that he wouldn't let you see, and there was a cold fire in his eyes. At the time there wasn't anything Paige could say. It was just a feeling she got when she was around him. Three months into their relationship, Amanda found out she was pregnant, and that Thomas had been sleeping with his lab partner on the side. In no time at all, he was out of the picture, much to the relief of Paige.

Amanda moved in with Paige and had a beautiful little girl that she named Lilly. She was such a happy child, innocent and beautiful-- all Amanda and nothing like her father. Both Paige and Amanda were happy about that. They continued to live with Paige and all three of them were happy with the way things were. It was just a few days after Lilly's fifth birthday that the plague struck and took Lilly.

The deflated remnants of balloons, the number five barely legible on their wrinkly rubber surface, still hung from the ceiling.

After the plague, Amanda clawed most of the decorations down, leaving long, blood-smeared lines on the walls. Paige had never seen her so feral or so fragile in her entire life.

Amanda didn't last very long after Lilly. The loss of a child was just too much for her. God knows how she did it-- how she managed to swallow that pint of bleach without her body instantly bringing it back up.

Paige blamed herself for what happened to Amanda, and she still did today. So, she vowed to herself that she was going to find out how the plague started. The plague had become her own personal enemy.

The buzzing of the phone on the desk brought Paige back to the present. Wiping the tears off her face, she picked up the receiver. The receptionist told her she had a call on line two. After the article she had just written, Paige knew she would have to field all kinds of calls from people calling her anything from a nut job to a conspiracy theorist. She said, "Okay," and switched over to line two.

"This is Paige Summers"

"Hello, Miss. My name is Mike Reynolds. I'm an EMT who was on duty the night the plague hit. I was wondering if we could meet sometime to go over the information you used in writing your article."

Something in this man's voice spoke of a genuine desire to learn the truth, and if he was an EMT on the night of the plague, he may have some information that she could use.

"What company do you work for?"

"It's an ambulance service called Life Express."

"I think I've seen your ambulances. Hang on a sec."

She opened up her calendar on her laptop to get an idea of what meetings she already had scheduled over the next week. "Ok, what's your schedule like over the next few days?"

"I start a three to eleven today. That leaves my mornings open for the next week," he answered.

She didn't have any meetings scheduled today, and the thought hit her that if she was in a meeting, she could tell the receptionist not to disturb her.

"Well, if you want to come by today, I have an open morning. Do you know how to get to my office?"

He chuckled. "Miss, I've been an ambulance driver for several years. There's not an address in Atlanta that I don't know how to get to."

"Yeah, I should have known that. Well, as I said, I'm free this morning, so let me know what time, and I'll put you on my schedule."

They both agreed on a little later that morning at around ten. Mike got his stuff together for the evening shift, made a pass at cleaning the house, and headed out.

The meeting with Ms. Summers wasn't for another hour. Mike knew it would take him around thirty minutes to get there so leaving now wouldn't put him too early.

At nine-thirty Mike was escorted into Paige's office. She glanced over at the man walking up to her desk. It was difficult to tell how old he was even as practiced as she was at observation. He had what they call salt and pepper hair and some wrinkles at the corner of his eyes. That was the only thing about him that spoke of any age.

"Thanks for agreeing to meet with me, Ms. Summers. I promise not to take up too much of your time. I know you must be very busy," he said as he walked over and took one of the seats across the desk from her. Mike was a little surprised with his first sight of Paige Summers, she was a great deal younger than he expected. In fact, she didn't seem much older than his daughter Sarah.

For her part, Paige was interested in hearing Mike tell his story of that night. Perhaps this would be another step towards finding the answers she was looking for. She glanced down at the note on her desk reminding her of his name. She had developed a habit of writing notes like this as a way to remember things. As fast-paced as her work was, this had become a very helpful habit.

"Mr. Reynolds, let me start by telling you that I have to protect my sources, so I hope you understand I can't reveal where any of my information comes from. You'll have to just believe me when I say that my sources are reliable. Are you okay with that?"

This wasn't unexpected by Mike, and he agreed with no hesitation.

"I would assume your editor has checked out your sources to make sure they are as correct as possible."

"Well, I checked them out. So you'll have to trust my information," Paige answered.

Mike had no problem in believing that the information Paige used was accurate. Only after his talk with Alter, he thought her conclusions were off track.

"One question I have is I would like to know any of the details that you have found out that maybe you didn't put in the story. The reason I would like to know is that I lost my family to the plague, and I have been looking at every bit of information I can to find some answers."

She thought for a few seconds before speaking again. "I can let you know this. A research scientist I spoke with is completely convinced that everyone on earth has been affected by whatever caused that plague. They have even looked into the possibility of a biological weapon going awry, but they haven't been able to find any evidence that would support that. According to this scientist, unless we find a way to reverse the effects of the plague, we are doomed. I have made calls to doctors all across the nation, and I am still yet to find a single pregnant woman anywhere in the U.S."

She had already given this information in her article, so Mike wasn't surprised to hear it. If Alter was right, then the earth had less than seven years from now before the end anyway. With every step he took, Mike was believing Alter more and more.

"I'm guessing you're not religious at all are you, Ms. Summers?"

"Are you?"

It was always Paige's standard operating procedure to answer a question like that with a question of her own. That way she would better know what direction the question was coming from and be mentally prepared.

"Well, until recently I thought I was. My family and I attended church regularly, but..."

"You gave it up for Lent?" she interrupted.

He just smiled and looked down. Paige decided to take advantage of his loss for words and do a little fishing for her own answers. "So, you were on duty the night of the plague. I would like to get some first account information. You probably saw more victims than anyone I know. Would you mind recounting the events of that night?"

This was a subject that tortured Mike almost every minute of every day. Even though he knew he would never grow numb to the pain, he had become used to it being part of him. He had learned to function with the pain. So, he was able to recount the events of that fateful night with almost clinical accuracy and attention to detail, at least until he got to the end of the night, and all he said was that his wife and daughter had also been taken by the plague.

His story confirmed part of what Paige had already learned. The plague victims had shown no signs of distress. It was like they were there, and then in a fraction of a second, they were gone.

That was one of the odd things Dr. Parks had told her they were so confused about. None of the autopsies showed a heart attack, stroke, or anything that would cause the victim to die like that. There was literally no reason for any of these people to be dead, but they were. She told this to Mike, and it puzzled her that he didn't show any surprise at all to this information.

"Mr. Reynolds, it seems to me that there is something that you're not telling me. Do you mind sharing with me what that is?"

Mike paused and looked down at the desk rather than looking Paige in the eye. "Ms. Summers, what information I have is going to be very difficult to explain, and I don't believe I should be giving my conclusions to a news reporter."

"May I call you Mike?" she asked. He nodded yes and she continued. "Mike, you and I both lost our family because of the plague. You're not here because I want to add to the story that I wrote. You're here, because above all else, I want to learn the truth. I promise you that nothing we talk about is going to end up in another story."

Paige was telling the truth, even more than she knew. She wasn't looking for another story. There was within her a force that was driving her to learn the truth about what happened.

There was something about the way Paige assured him that this was not going to turn into another story that made Mike believe her, so he agreed to tell her everything. He told her that this was going to take some due diligence on her part. He said he could meet her in a couple of days with some background information for her to study. He warned her that she would need an open mind and not to jump to any judgments or conclusions until she had seen all the information.

"You know, it sounds like you are asking me to 'suspend my disbelief,' to quote a politician," she said.

"In a way, I guess I am. What I'm really asking you is, are you willing to believe what's right in front of you?" Mike answered.

There was something in the simple direct way he spoke that caused Paige to agree with his request. So, they scheduled another time to meet in two days.

Mike asked for a couple of days before he brought her the information because he wanted to give himself tonight and tomorrow to talk to Alter and maybe have him come along in the near future and speak with Paige.

When Mike got to work later that afternoon, he saw Alter and handed him the magazine with the article Paige Summers wrote. "I found this and once I read it, I thought of you. I also met with the girl who wrote the article. It may be useful for you to meet her as well."

Alter glanced at the magazine when Mike handed it to him, but his expression changed when he heard that Mike wanted him to meet her as well. Then he motioned Mike to come with him out of hearing distance of the others.

"Mike, when things start moving forward, we won't be able to trust anyone. The only reason I trusted you was that I believe I was led to talk to you."

Mike wasn't fazed. "I understand and I can't explain it, but for some reason, I believe we can trust this girl."

Alter wasn't so sure about trusting anyone at this point. Ben had done a great deal of studying on the seven-year period after the church is called home. After reading the notes Ben had recorded and some of the books he had referenced, Alter believed that surviving the next seven years was going to be quite a stretch. When he read about families betraying each other, he just didn't know about trusting someone just because Mike did. Even with all his doubts, something inside him made him want to trust Mike's judgment, so he relented.

"Ok, I'll trust your instincts with this one. I take it that you have done some recon of your own, and you believe me."

"Yes. Could we talk a bit after the shift tonight?"

Alter agreed and said he would come over to Mike's house after the shift. From that point, the two of them were focused on the calls that came in throughout the rest of the shift.

One thing that had changed at Life Express other than smaller crews on each shift was that each ambulance had to move a great deal more cautiously when they were on a run. It seemed that even though the population had decreased, the gang activity had increased dramatically. That, coupled with a diminished police force, increased the danger on each run. It had gotten to where there was no difference in neighborhoods. Mike was glad he lived outside of Metro Atlanta where there were fewer people and fewer problems. It almost felt strange to be glad of anything, but recently he had a small unexplainable sense of hope. He actually looked forward to the day when he would be reunited with his family and he knew that no matter how hard his life became, that reunion was in the foreseeable future.

When their shift was over, Alter drove straight to Mike's home and the two of them went to the kitchen table and sat down. It was eleven-thirty at night and neither one of them wanted coffee so Alter pulled out his laptop.

Alter told Mike that he was going to trust his instincts where this girl was concerned, and also he had read the article Mike had given him.

"So, what did you think about her story?" Mike asked.

Alter paused only briefly before answering. "It does seem that she is looking for truth, but I'm afraid that the more she learns and understands the truth, the harder it's going to be for her."

"I'm not sure I understand what you mean."

"Her sister wasn't taken like her niece. Her sister committed suicide. She died without the Messiah."

Suddenly the reality of what Alter said hit Mike like a ton of bricks.

"That's not something we have to mention to her."

"No, we will not bring the subject up, but if she asks something, I'm going to have to be honest."

With that settled, the two of them moved on to talk about how much information to give Paige to look over. They didn't want to overwhelm her with too much information, but at the same time they wanted to give her enough so she could draw a logical conclusion. They both agreed that this was going to be difficult. Mike knew that in his own case, he had a bank of teachings from the past that he could use. Paige had a completely different background, and that made it a challenge to decide where to start. In the end, they decided to start with the foretelling of the coming of Christ and the mathematical impossibility of someone fulfilling all of those prophecies. Beyond that, Mike thought that it would take face-to-face conversations, possibly a lot of them. At this point, Mike was beginning to doubt his belief that talking to Paige Summers was a good idea. Alter assured him that originally he had his own doubts about sharing this information with Mike, and even though things were going to get more difficult, he thought Mike had done the right thing in meeting Ms. Summers.

"Just how difficult do you think things are going to get?" Mike asked, not really wanting to know.

"I think things are going to get very bad, but I'm no Bible scholar."

"Well, at this point, I don't think I would trust a Bible scholar. If someone claims to be a Bible scholar and they were not taken, then I would have a hard time believing anything they said, so I'm thinking we will have to trust each other," Mike answered.

They put together the files they thought would be best for Paige to start with, and at a glance the files seemed pretty lengthy. Mike called Paige's office and confirmed the time and place for them to get together so he could pass on the information to her.

They met at an out-of-the-way diner called Annie's. It was one of the many diners in the south that advertised their home-cooked meals. It was also a diner that was not near the magazine Paige worked for or Life Express, which made it unlikely someone would recognize them.

Once at the diner Mike chose a table that was by itself so people wouldn't be tempted to listen to their conversation. He ordered a cup of coffee and a slice of apple pie. Paige arrived at the diner before the waitress made it back with his coffee and pie. Mike saw her come into the diner and he waved her over to his table. She came to the table and took the seat across from him.

"Thanks for meeting me here today. I've got some coffee and a slice of pie on the way. What would you like? My treat."

"I'll have the same, thanks."

Just at that point, the waitress came by with Mike's order.

"Thanks. Could you bring out the same for the young lady, on the same ticket?"

The waitress looked at Paige. "Do you want anything in the coffee?"

"Just some cream, thanks."

When the waitress walked off to place the order, Mike slid a thumb drive across the table to Paige.

"Here's the first of the information I have for you. It may take you a few days to go through it all, and at first, it's almost going to feel like a complete waste of time. Please commit to going through everything and know that there is more. Much more."

Just then the waitress came back with Paige's coffee and pie. "I'll check back with you to see if you want your coffee warmed up," she said as she started to leave.

Paige took a bite of the pie, closed her eyes for a second, and then looked at Mike. "This is really good. Do you eat here often?"

"Nope, this is my first visit, I just picked it because I like the location."

"Mr. Reynolds, I get this feeling that there's something you're not telling me."

Mike took that moment to taste the pie himself. To Paige that seemed like an obvious stalling tactic. Mike wasn't trying to stall for time. He had already decided to be very open with her. So, once he took a bite himself, he answered her right away. "You're right. There are some things I haven't told you yet, but I think, that like me, you will need to see the information in an order that makes sense."

His answer didn't exactly make sense to her, but she decided to wait and see what was on that thumb drive. She couldn't tell if it was just that she felt some sort of kinship with him because of their shared losses or if it was his direct matter-of-fact manner that made her trust him. Maybe it was something else altogether, but whatever it was, she found herself trusting him. Paige had already guessed from his avoidance of the subject that he deeply missed his wife and daughter, probably as much as she missed her sister and niece. Mike mentioned to her that his daughter was just a little younger than she was. That meant that he and his wife had been together for more than twenty years. That kind of loss was more than she could imagine. To be together that long took more than commitment. That took a kind of love that few people had.

They set a date and time to meet back at this restaurant again. Paige had a few days to look over the file and Mike had some time to make a plan with Alter on how to explain what they now believed.

CHAPTER EIGHT

P RIME Minister Marco Corsetti and his entourage arrived at the Colosseum well before the Israeli Prime Minister did. This was not his habit. He normally would arrive at a scheduled meeting with an official from another country almost half an hour late or more. Subconsciously that would tell the official that they really weren't all that important to him or his agenda. In this case, however, he wanted Israel to feel important and needed. As far as Marco was concerned, they were needed, but in his mind, they were more of a means to an end.

There was a large and elaborate tent set up on the floor of the arena the day before. It had been built specifically for this meeting. The inside of the tent was a meticulously furnished board room. Once inside there was no way to tell that it wasn't part of a grand building rather than a tent sitting on the arena floor of the Roman Colosseum. It was complete with hardwood floors and immaculate furnishing. Stepping inside was like walking into a completely different world.

During the famous Roman Empire, this was a place where so much blood had been spilled that the smell coming up from the blood-soaked dirt floor had been almost overpowering.

Notified of the arrival of the Israeli Prime Minister, Corsetti dismissed his aids and stood at the end of the conference table nearest to the door. He had a very calm, confident demeanor that spoke of a deep strength and power that could be seen by even the most casual observation.

The Prime Minister of Israel, Ephraim Bar Aaron, along with two of his aides, were escorted into the meeting. Corsetti walked forward with a warm smile and offered his hand to Bar Aaron. The two of them shook hands and then had a seat at the table, Corsetti at the end of the table with Bar Aaron on the side immediately to his left.

"You seem to have made quite a lot of progress in a very short period of time in bringing all these countries under one government. It is very impressive," said Bar Aaron.

Corsetti smiled. "It has been a whirlwind of activity. One thing that has helped immensely is that all the nations have voluntarily come together. If it had been some kind of military coup, then I'm sure we would have been thrown into a period of chaos that would have lasted for years. Not to change the subject but, a great many civilizations have been crippled by the plague that hit the world. How has Israel faired through this?"

"We were affected by the plague, but we were not hit as hard as many other nations. In many respects, our nation has been able to maintain things the way they were before the plague."

The meeting went on smoothly with the two of them verbally agreeing to a mutually beneficial alliance as well as having a formal meeting on a treaty between Israel and The New World Order.

At the end of their conversation, Marco offered to give the Prime Minister a tour of the Colosseum, which was accepted, and the two of them along with a large entourage headed out.

Since he was a child, Marco had always been fascinated with the ancient Roman empire. He especially admired the rule of Augustus that ushered in the famous Pax Romana, which brought in two centuries of peace and prosperity to the Roman empire. Now, as an adult, he could see the cause of the eventual downfall of Rome, and he believed that if Rome were to rise again, it could be established in a way that it would not suffer that same fate.

The tour took them outside to the different arches that had been built in honor of different Roman heroes. Marco headed toward the Arch of Titus almost immediately.

Ephraim Bar Aaron stopped in his tracks as soon as he realized where they were headed. "Excuse me Prime Minister, but that is one arch I really don't need to see," he said.

Marco turned and feigned a show of surprise. "Is something wrong, my friend?"

Bar Aaron pointed toward the Arch of Titus and explained his reluctance to go over there.

"That is the Arch of Titus, and the Talmud forbids a Jew to be under that arch. The emperor Titus used twenty thousand Jewish slaves to build the Colosseum. Even though that was thousands of years ago, and I am not as devout a Jew as many others, I still cannot go against our Talmud so brazenly."

That was the exact reaction Marco was hoping for. "I am so sorry, I did not mean any offense, we can go the opposite direction of course."

With that, he headed back towards the Colosseum. Bar Aaron followed and they continued with the tour. As the day came to an end, he walked with the Israeli prime minister back to the limo he had arrived in.

"Ephraim, there's been something on my mind since we saw the Arch of Titus earlier today. I would like to do something as a show of our mutual friendship. I cannot erase the offenses of Titus, but I think there is a gesture your people would appreciate."

Bar Aaron turned and waited to hear what Marco was about to suggest.

"What I would like to do is have my engineers and architects work with your priests to rebuild the Jewish temple right back on its original site."

The Israeli smiled with almost the same expression that an adult would have when their child announces that they are going to build a spaceship and fly to the moon.

"I do appreciate the thought but I'm afraid something like that is out of the question."

"Let me assure you that my people would be completely under the direction of the priests."

Bar Aaron shook his head slightly. "The problem is the location of the original temple. That spot is where The Dome of the Rock is located, and it has been there for over thirteen hundred years. As you know the location is considered sacred by the Muslims. Israel is utterly dedicated to preserving the Holy Places in a territory it controls, for all religions."

Nothing else was said by either man for what seemed like forever, then an idea came to Marco. "I would very much like our next meeting to be in Israel and if it can be arranged, I would also like to meet with the leaders of your religion."

The Israeli leader said that it would be an honor for their next meeting to be held in Israel and suggested that when the meeting happened Marco might want to refer to the Rabbi as Rabbi rather than Priest.

"Oh yes, I always get them mixed up, priest, rabbi, imam. I definitely will not make that mistake again. I promise, you will have nothing to worry about."

Their initial meeting ended with the agreement that the next meeting would be in Israel with Marco having a chance to meet and speak with a rabbi.

Marco headed back to his office knowing what his next move would be. This day had gone exactly as he had planned. On the limo ride back to his office, Marco reached over and turned off the communication line between him and his driver to make sure that his next phone call would not be accidentally overheard. He pulled out his cell and dialed a number that wasn't in his phone's memory. A man's voice answered.

"I'm in Rome, we need to talk."

"Sorry, you must have the wrong number," the man said and then hung up. That was a code he and Marco had come up with. Had he said anything else, they would try again in exactly twenty-four hours with another prearranged code.

The man's name was Lorenzo Russo. He and Marco had known each other since they were boys in school. Their friendship had started when Marco was only in the fifth grade. During recess, the class bully decided that Marco was his next target. The bully's name was Luca, and he had been held back a year. Luca was already rather big for his age, and he was a year older than any of the others. That almost made him a natural bully.

Marco was sitting at a picnic table, minding his own business, working on a crossword puzzle. Then, for no apparent reason, Luca walked over and started to tease Marco. He grabbed the crossword book with one hand and with the other pushed Marco off the bench to the ground. Marco stood up knowing that he was no match for Luca physically, but he also knew he could completely humiliate this boy verbally and make him wish that he had never messed with Marco Corsetti.

Then something happened that took Marco completely by surprise.

"Give him the book back and walk away."

That was Lorenzo Russo, the boy Marco had helped with his math work earlier that week.

Lorenzo was very soft-spoken and almost never made his presence known to those around him. He was someone that just went unnoticed by most people. What people didn't know was that Lorenzo's father was an instructor of Aiki Jujitsu and had been working with Lorenzo since he was only five years old. To the casual observer, the style was similar to Aikido, but only to the casual observer. In reality, it was a much older and much more violent style of martial art.

Luca held up the book, smiled, and then tore it in half and threw the two halves toward Marco. Without saying another word, Lorenzo walked over towards Luca, who instantly reached out to grab the smaller boy. Lorenzo sidestepped the attempted grab and stomped down on the boy's instep, while at the same time he put Luca into an armbar.

Luca went down to his knees in pain from the kick to the instep as well as the pressure being applied to both his wrist and elbow. "OK, I'll leave him alone."

"Oh, yes, you most certainly will." Lorenzo answered him.

Then in the next instant, he brought all of his weight down on the bigger boy's twisted elbow, and there was a loud sickening sound of a bone cracking.

Luca screamed.

The teachers were on the scene in an instant and took Lorenzo to the administrator's office. Had it not been for Marco following and then speaking to the administrator that would have been Lorenzo's last day at school. Marco told the administrator that Lorenzo had just stepped in to try and stop Luca from harassing him. When he tried to get the book back, the two of them fell to the ground wrestling for it, and somehow in the fall, Luca's arm snapped.

In the end, they believed Marco's version of what happened over what Luca had said because Luca was well known as a bully, while Lorenzo had never caused any problems before.

Lorenzo did get two weeks of detention that were over in what seemed like no time at all. From that point forward Marco and Lorenzo were fast friends.

That incident at school and what happened later in the administrator's office taught Marco a valuable lesson on the power of persuasion and how he could use it to his advantage. Marco began to study people and how to manipulate them using psychology to get them to see things the way he wanted them to see them. He found that there is more power in the ability to convince people than there is in an entire military force. It's one thing to be able to force someone to do something. It's completely different to have them want to do it.

Lorenzo's interests led him in a completely different direction. Lorenzo's father had always taught him that, if he did get into any kind of altercation, he was to make sure that he would not be followed when he started to walk away. That meant to take away the ability of the other person to follow in any way. Moving from hand-to-hand techniques to guns just seemed to be a natural step.

When they got older, Marco went into politics, while Lorenzo chose a very different line of work. Through the years they kept in touch with each other, and Marco, on some occasions, found a need for Lorenzo's special services.

To say that Lorenzo was a hitman, would be akin to saying that Michaelangelo was just another artist. Lorenzo had a very special skill set, and over the years he had acquired an impressive set of tools along with an equally impressive list of contacts.

Today Marco was facing a very unusual challenge, and he believed he needed every resource he could call on for this one. The driver took him to his home in Italy. It was a breath-taking estate on the top of a hill overlooking Lake Albano. Once there, he dismissed the driver. Marco waited until the driver was well gone before he went to one of the auto garages and entered the code for the electronic garage door lock. The garage housed five cars that were well maintained by his staff. One of the cars was a nondescript Alpha Romero which he chose because in Rome that was the type of car that no one ever paid attention to. Less than a minute later, he was on the road headed towards his meeting with Lorenzo. On the drive, he thought about his objectives and how he might accomplish them. Within twenty minutes he arrived at his destination, a small villa hidden away in the country well off the beaten track of both tourists and locals. There was no vehicle in sight, but that meant nothing. Lorenzo was likely sitting inside waiting for him.

Marco parked his car, got out, and walked to the front door. He tried the doorknob, and to no surprise, it was unlocked. As he opened the door, Lorenzo got up from the sofa he had been sitting on, walked over, and greeted his friend. "Ciao, Amico."

Whenever they were together, both of them immediately moved to their native language of Italian.

"The last time we met you were simply the Prime Minister of Italy. Look at you now. I don't even know what to call you. Should it be Prime Minister or your Majesty?"

"I think for you, Marco will be perfect."

Lorenzo motioned for his friend to have a seat in an armchair facing the sofa as he returned to the sofa. Marco nodded and sat in the plush armchair.

"I don't have any spiced wine to offer you, but I do have some nice Pinot Noir." Lorenzo didn't wait for Marco to answer him. Instead, he walked over to the counter where he had a wine serving set, filled two glasses, and brought one to Marco. "So, what is it that you need from me?"

Marco took a sip of his wine and leaned back in the chair. He explained his idea of developing a relationship with Israel by initiating the building of their temple. He told Lorenzo that one thing standing in his way was the presence of the Muslim temple, The Dome of the Rock.

"I don't understand why you are wanting to do this. Have you suddenly become religious since forming The New World Order?"

Marco chuckled at his friend's comments. "I am after two objectives. By building this temple, we will replace America as the Savior of Israel, and that will make a treaty with America much easier. Even though they were crippled by the plague, America is still a force I would like to have a controlling interest in."

The two of them talked for the next few hours about the challenges Marco was facing and the possible answers to those challenges. The answer they agreed on would be difficult to accomplish. There was also the possibility of it going wrong in many ways, but in the end, it seemed to be the one path that would work. It was going to take serious planning and preparation by Lorenzo. He assured Marco that he would put all of his attention to the task. "Keep me updated on when things will begin."

"Oh, you will have to be in the know, because you will have a significant part to play, and the timing will be crucial."

CHAPTER NINE

To say that the meeting with Mike Reynolds was strange would be an understatement. He did seem to be searching for answers just like she was. Paige hoped that he wasn't a weirdo who was going to try to convince her that what happened was some sort of alien invasion or something, but there was something about the man that made her want to trust him. Even so, she also wanted to be careful of not being desperate enough to fall for anything.

She had finished her day at the office and was sitting at home caught somewhere between medicating her sense of loss with a bottle of Jim Beam and getting started on the files she had been given by Mike Reynolds. After some internal debate, going over the file with a cup of coffee won out. She made the decision right then that it was time to stop numbing herself. She wasn't going to become a statistic. She felt as if Amanda, her sister, had given up when she ended her life and there were moments when she was angry about that. Amanda's memory still haunted her daily, giving her a never-ending drive to find out the truth. There had to be a reason for all of this, and she wasn't going to quit until she found out what it was.

Paige walked into the kitchen and started a pot of coffee. While she waited for it to brew, she took her laptop into her home office, plugged it in, and turned it on. Upon inserting the thumb drive and opening it up, she saw that it had several files. She opened the file that said "proof". It had a few word docs, and she started with the one on the top left. Before getting too enthralled, she decided to go and wait in the kitchen for the coffee to finish brewing. Paige knew herself well enough to know that once she started working on a project, she would forget all about the coffee that would be sitting in the kitchen for her.

Within a few minutes, she was sitting at her desk with a fresh cup of coffee on her left and a notepad to her right.

The following is proof that my people were, and but for a few exceptions, still are, wrong about the coming Messiah. The notes contained in this research will prove beyond a shadow of a doubt that the Jesus of the Christians is in fact the Messiah we Jews have been waiting for.

After reading the short intro, Paige couldn't help but wonder if Mike had mistakenly given her the wrong thumb drive. This research obviously had nothing to do with the plague that had devastated the world. That's when she remembered that Mike had told her the information would seem like a waste of time at first, but that by the end it all tied together. She figured she would go on if for no other reason than to find out what had him convinced that he had found some answers. She glanced down at the number of pages on the document and saw what Mr. Reynolds had meant when he told her that it would take her a while to go through all the files. If this document was any indication of how much was on the thumb drive, it was going to take her a good bit of time to go over all of it. She thought she could at least get the idea of where it was headed by skimming through what she could.

A significant Messianic prophecy that is often overlooked by those still waiting for the Messiah is Daniel 9:24–27. This Old Testament prophecy says that Messiah, the Anointed One, will be "cut off," or killed, before the destruction of the Temple in Jerusalem, which happened in 70 A.D. Clearly, Yeshua's death fits as fulfilling this prophecy, and no Messiah yet to come could. Bible prophecy contains portraits of both a suffering Messiah and a victorious Messiah. The suffering servant is pictured as a lamb, wounded, and cut off, but not for Himself. The triumphant Messiah comes to establish His rule of peace and righteousness over the earth.

These two seemingly contradictory prophetic descriptions are difficult to understand for Jewish People. To reconcile these two very different portrayals of the Messiah, there grew a belief among the rabbis that they were waiting for two Messiahs. One they called Mashiach ben David, and He would be the Son of King David who would rule and reign. The other they called Mashiach ben Joseph, the Son of Joseph. This Messiah ben Joseph would suffer and be rejected by his own, like Joseph was rejected by his brothers. At the time of Yeshua's coming, Israel longed for the conquering Messiah. Because of Rome's oppression and their expectation that God would send the Deliverer, they were looking for Yeshua ben David.

The truth is, it is not two Messiahs-- it is one Messiah coming twice. First as the Lamb of God, the suffering servant of Isaiah 53, and then as the reigning King Messiah when Yeshua returns. Yeshua's first coming fulfilled the prophecies of the suffering servant. With Yeshua's Second Coming, we will see the fulfillment of the victorious, reigning Messiah of Isaiah 11:1–9!

One thing the writer said that got her attention and stuck with her in a way she could not shake off, was when he started talking about the law of probability. In probability theory, the law (or formula) of total probability is a fundamental rule relating marginal probabilities to conditional probabilities. It expresses the total probability of an outcome that can be realized via several distinct events--hence the name. Broken down, the law of total probability could give the percentage chance for the desired outcome of any event. Going by the math, it was more than impossible for Jesus to have fulfilled the prophecies that he did. That just couldn't have happened, yet according to the research, more than three hundred of those prophecies were fulfilled through the life of one man.

"Why don't the preachers make information like this available? If they did, it would cause their churches to fill up," she said to herself out loud.

For a brief period, Paige dated a guy who had ambitions of being a professional gambler. He was the one who had first gotten her interested in the law of probability. He was studying the odds of a winning hand and he had decided the best overall odds were when he was playing Blackjack. That got her interested and she started by studying averages which led her to the law of probability. The relationship didn't last very long. He ended up seeing some girl who worked in a casino on the coast. Paige laughed, wondering what the odds of that were.

The fact that Jesus of Nazareth actually fulfilled that many prophecies, most of which were over four hundred years before his birth, was staggering to her.

As interesting as all this was, she still had no idea why she had been given this file.

Paige looked at the time at the bottom of her screen. She was surprised to see that she had been reading for almost three hours. Her coffee was cold, and she suddenly realized how tired she was, so she shut the laptop down and headed towards her bedroom. Before she went to sleep, Paige made a mental note to call Mike Reynolds and ask him to meet her earlier than the meeting they had talked about.

It was only the second day after he met with Paige Summers that Mike got a call on his cell phone, with Paige asking to move up their scheduled meeting. Mike wanted to talk to Alter and let him know about the change, so he told her that he could call her back in a few minutes to let her know.

Alter was out on a call, and it was likely Mike would get a run before Alter made it back. That was the way these shifts had always been. The team didn't see each other unless it was at the beginning or end of a shift. They mainly just spent the entire shift with the person they were partnered up with. Mike sent Alter a text asking him to call when he got a minute. Then after thinking about it, he sent another text letting him know that Paige Summers called to ask if she could meet him earlier than they had planned. In the next sentence, he asked Alter if he would be okay with either tonight or tomorrow night after their shift.

It only took a minute before his phone chimed. Alter had answered his text saying that either night would work with him. Mike took no time at all from then calling Paige Summers back.

"This is Paige," came the voice in a crisp business-like tone.

"Hi, Ms. Summers. This is Mike Reynolds calling you back. I needed to run a couple of options by you."

"Sure, go ahead."

"OK, well as you know I'm an EMT and our company runs a little different than any other company I know of. Instead of the traditional twenty-four on twenty-four off, we work in eight-hour shifts. Right now, I'm in the middle of a swing shift."

"Sorry, I don't know what you mean by a swing shift," Paige answered.

"A swing shift is when we work from three in the afternoon until eleven that night. So, I can meet you tonight or tomorrow night, but it will have to be eleven-thirty or midnight."

Sleep wasn't something Paige got much of these days, so meeting at midnight didn't bother her. The diner where they had first met would be closed, so they chose an IHOP that they both knew about. Mike told her that he couldn't control what emergency was going to happen or when it might happen, so he would call her if it looked like he couldn't make it.

At her office, it seemed Paige was being reprimanded because she had been taken off the schedule as a journalist and had been moved into a position of proofreading and correcting other people's stories. She knew this hadn't come from her editor because he had approved her story before it went into print. Part of her was insulted and another part was glad for the ability to continue chasing down leads, like Mike Reynolds. She arrived at the IHOP at eleven-thirty sharp, went in, and ordered a cup of decaf. She hadn't received a text or call from Mike saying that he wouldn't make it or that he would be late, so she assumed he would arrive within the next few minutes.

She was a bit surprised when he arrived because he had someone with him. It was another man about Mike's age, dressed in the same EMT uniform as Mike. He had the black hair and the olive skin tone of someone from the Middle East.

"Hello, Ms. Summers. I would like you to meet my friend Alter Cagan. He's the source of the information I gave you."

Paige and Alter shook hands and everyone sat down. Each of the two men ordered a stack of pancakes and a cup of coffee. Paige had noticed this trait among emergency workers and had wondered about it. One day she asked a man why people in any kind of work like that seemed to have that habit. He explained that it originated on the battlefield with the military since you never knew when your next meal would be, you ate as much as you could when you had the opportunity. She saw how that could translate over to emergency personnel fairly easily. "Your name is Alter? That's a fairly unusual name. Where does it come from?" she asked.

"It's Hebrew. My family came to this country from Israel when I was a child."

"So, you are Jewish, I guess?"

Alter smiled and looked at Mike. "I guess if you are looking for a title, then I am what used to be known as a Messianic Jew, and I believe that Jews all over the world are beginning to wake up to this new reality."

Hearing the way he said that made Paige think that if she didn't get control of this conversation quickly there was no telling where it would end up. "I don't want to be rude, but, Mr. Reynolds, you led me to believe that you had some answers about how this plague hit," she said, emphasizing the word plague. "That's why I agreed to meet you the first time. When we met, you were fairly cryptic in what you said, and you gave me all this research your friend here did. As interesting as the research may be, I fail to see how it can contain any answers about the plague."

About that time the pancakes arrived. The waitress placed a plate in front of each man and asked if anybody needed anything. When they said they didn't, she smiled and left them alone.

Alter was the first to speak after the waitress left. "Miss, I need to start by letting you know that I am not the one who did that research. It was done by a good friend of mine who is no longer with us. He was one of those we lost to the plague."

"I'm sorry for your loss, but I still don't see how that research can give me any kind of clue as to what has happened." Paige empathized with his pain, but she wasn't going to be sidetracked.

"I will explain. It will take some time and you will want to do some investigation, I'm sure. In the end, it will be worth the time and effort," Alter said, while taking his first bite of pancake. Paige motioned to the waitress and asked for a smaller order of pancakes and a refill of her coffee. Then she looked at Alter and motioned for him to continue. He chuckled to himself realizing that she was telling him by her actions that she was giving him what he asked for. At first, he was at a loss as to how to begin.

"I will start with what we are calling the plague. I don't believe those who are gone were the victims. I believe they are the only true survivors, and we are the victims. I can see by the expression on your face that you think I'm one of those crazies, but please bear with me. I've got a lot to explain."

The waitress arrived with Paige's pancakes and refilled her cup. Paige was beginning to think that maybe she was the one who was crazy to be sitting here eating breakfast at midnight with two strangers listening to this crap. She took a bite of pancake and motioned for Alter to continue.

"You see, Ms. Summers, my friend, the one who did the research, was also a Jew, and the research he did was what convinced him that as a Jew, he had been wrong about the prophecies of the Messiah. Because of that, he converted to Christianity. If you continue to read those files you will see the undeniable evidence that caused him to accept Jesus Christ as his savior."

Paige listened to what Alter said and thought to herself that since Alter's friend had died in the plague, he hadn't been saved from anything.

"There are still some prophecies that are being fulfilled as we speak. One of those was the taking away of God's children. The people who you believe died in the plague, I don't believe they died, but that they were called home and now have a new body and they will live for eternity. I believe that we are now living in the time that was foretold as the great tribulation, and it will last for seven years."

Well, that confirmed it for her. She was crazy to be sitting here with these two. Paige excused herself and got up to leave.

"Ms. Summers." Mike got her attention just as she was starting to walk away.

"Before you go, let me say one thing. Watch on the news. There will soon be a worldwide government established, and when that happens, things will start spiraling down very quickly. It has been foretold in prophecies thousands of years ago. When you see this happen, you may want to get in touch with us."

CHAPTER TEN

U MAR ibn Bakr had served as Caliph for several years, and it had been a stress-free period other than the normal tensions with the Jews, which had become rare. His oldest son was an engineer, and his two daughters were at University. Allah had been good to him. Many others had been shamed by their children's blatant disregard of Islamic law.

His assistant came to him with a phone receiver in his hand. "It's your wife, sir. She said that it is important that she speak with you." The assistant handed him the phone and left the room. A slight wave of concern went through him as he put the phone to his ear. It wasn't like her to call while he was at work, so this had to mean that something was wrong.

"Hello?"

The voice on the other end of the line was not his wife. It was a man. "This call is to give you the foreknowledge that you will need so you can make the right decisions in the very near future."

"Who is this?" Umar demanded as the wave of concern turned into the edge of fear.

"Your wife just died of a heart attack, and no one will be able to prove her death was anything other than a natural event. In less than a week the Dome of the Rock will be destroyed by a series of explosions. You will follow my instructions with no exceptions, or the rest of your family will systematically die as well. When you find your wife's body at your home, you will also find a cell phone. You are to keep that phone on your person at all times. That is where you will receive your instructions."

The line suddenly went dead. The fear that hit Umar produced an acidic taste in his mouth. He stood up to leave and the room started to spin around him. He grabbed the desk to steady himself and keep from falling. His assistant in the other room saw him swaying and came to him immediately.

"Sir, may I help?" His concern for the Caliph was evident.

"I need to go home immediately."

Umar allowed his assistant to help him out to a car and help him into the back seat. His assistant got into the driver's seat, and they headed to the home of the Caliph.

The home was built of adobe with multiple decks surrounding it and gates that opened automatically from a remote in the car. Once inside the gate, Umar opened his door and rushed into the house. His wife was in the sitting room on the floor with her cell phone next to her hand. The assistant was only seconds behind him, and upon seeing the scene, he immediately called for an ambulance. Umar reached down to pick up his wife and the assistant gently stopped him.

"We don't know if moving her will cause more damage. We should wait for the emergency technicians to arrive."

It only took a few minutes for the ambulance to arrive. The technicians were only there for a few minutes before pronouncing her dead at the scene. They asked the Caliph to have a seat so the police could get his statement.

The details of the conversation he had had just minutes before with the man on the phone went through his mind. He didn't think the man could do what he had threatened, but he did believe his family was in danger. He told the police that he felt like something was wrong when his wife had called, so he had his assistant take him home where the two of them found her. He said he wanted them to do everything they could without desecrating the body to determine whether or not her death was from natural causes. He told his assistant to go ahead without him, as he was going to stay at home waiting to hear from the doctor.

When everyone had left, leaving him alone at his home, Umar felt lost in his own home. He knew that he was going to have to gather the strength to let his children know what had happened to their mother. He went up the stairs and went into his bedroom. On the nightstand next to his bed was a cell phone with a charger next to it. He knew the phone had been left there for him to find. He picked up the phone and charger and put them in the breast pocket of his suit jacket. Then he called his assistant and asked him to bring his children to his home. He did not want them to find out over the phone or by watching the news report that would surely be broadcast soon. They deserved to be told in person by him.

In his own way, Umar did love his wife. She had been a good woman who had never tried to interject herself into his public life, and she had never protested him taking his pleasure with other women.

Later that afternoon, his three children were brought to the house, where he told them that their mother had died earlier that day of a heart attack. All three of them were devastated by the news. All three of them took time off from work and school to be with their father and help him with the arrangements for the funeral the next day. Islamic tradition was that the burial was to take place within twenty-four hours of death for sanitary reasons.

The man who spoke to Umar on the phone had been hired by Lorenzo Russo. Three of them had disabled the alarm system of the house using an electronic device that used a universal code to shut the alarm down. They entered the house without any fear of detection, found the woman they were looking for in the sitting room, made her call her husband at gunpoint, and then one of them took the phone away from her while the other two forced her to swallow a liquid made from aconite.

Aconite was a highly toxic plant that had been used to produce medicine in China. It was also known as Wolfsbane or Queen of Poison. It could be detected with the type of autopsy done in the west, but because of Islamic tradition, her death, which would be painful but quick, would be deemed a natural heart attack.

Several days before the team was sent to the Caliph's home, another team had been assembled. This was a team of Pakistani recruits whose job was to place charges in predetermined areas around the temple. Since they were from Pakistan and were apparently Muslim, they were free to carry out their assignments without raising any security alarms. All of the charges were radio controlled and were strategically placed in areas that would cause complete destruction of the Dome. There would definitely be deaths from the explosion, but the number of deaths would be determined by what time the explosions happened.

Four days after the death of Umar's wife the Muslim world was rocked by the terrorist attack that destroyed the Dome of the Rock. Less than an hour after the news broke, the phone that the Caliph had found on the nightstand next to his bed began to vibrate. Everyone in the room was so focused on speculation of who attacked and how it was done, no one noticed or paid attention when the Caliph walked away with the phone to his ear. He heard a different voice from the one who had spoken to him the day his wife died. Both times the man spoke English. The first time, however, it had been a broken English. This time it was perfect English with a very distinct accent, possibly Italian.

"Thank you for answering so promptly. Now here is what you will do next. You will announce that an extensive investigation is underway to determine who is responsible for this travesty. You will also pledge to rebuild the temple. You will, however, change the location of the temple. Then you will turn over the rights of the current location to Israel to do whatever they want."

Umar could not do what this mad man was telling him. The people would revolt, and he would be removed as Caliph.

"What you are asking is impossible, it cannot be done."

Then the man's voice spoke again with an unnerving calm. "I believe that I need to explain your predicament. You are only going to be told this once. If you do not comply, every one of your children will die in front of you, and then you will die, and I will simply move on to your successor."

Umar took a second to speak. Whoever this was, he had proved what he was capable of. For the first time in his life he was terrified. "I will do what you ask, but what if I fail?"

"Don't fail."

The line went dead.

CHAPTER ELEVEN

T HE news report was on every station all over the world. Terrorists had set explosions and destroyed a Muslim temple called The Dome of the Rock. The report stated that over two hundred worshipers were killed in the explosion. The Caliph from Pakistan made a brief statement saying that their people were working with the Israeli investigators to determine who was behind this attack. He also made a statement saying that the rebuilding of the temple was going to take place in a new location where it could be better protected by the Muslim community. The part of the story that really caught Paige's attention was when the Prime Minister of The New World Order made a statement offering any support that was needed.

The Prime Minister of the New World Order. She had seen a report on this New World Order before. It had begun with the dissolving of the European Union. The individual countries had come together under one government and had their own type of electronic currency. When the report had come out, she had mostly ignored it because it didn't affect the United States and because she was dealing with her own issues. Looking at things now and remembering that statement made by Mike Reynolds as she was leaving the IHOP made her uneasy. She was curious what Mike and his friend would have to say about the news report she just saw and what their thoughts would be on this New World Order. She decided not to call Mike Reynolds because, at this point, she considered the two of them almost in the same category as conspiracy theorists. Rather than call and get their opinions, she was sure that she could get the answers for herself.

Paige suddenly got a call from the editor. Hoping that she was about to get her position as journalist back, she got up and went straight to her editor's office. Her editor was Jim Boyles, an old school journalist who she had worked with for a few years. He was one of those who had built his career as a bulldog for the truth, no matter what the consequences. He had not been in the office for the last few days, so she was going to go talk to him as soon as she got a chance anyway. She walked into Boyles' office where he was sitting at his desk. Boyles always looked unkempt, but he looked even more so today. He was an overweight man with thinning hair. He normally wore a suit without a tie. Today he was in a short-sleeve button-up shirt that was untucked. There was an ashtray on his desk with a lit cigarette sitting in it. He glanced up when she walked in.

"You about ready to be a journalist again?" he asked as he looked back down at his work on the desk.

"Absolutely"

He motioned for her to sit down, and she did.

"Your first task is real simple. I want you to print a retraction of the story you wrote. Do it any way you want but make it good and believable."

Paige couldn't believe she was being asked to write a retraction. She had been a professional journalist for almost three years. Before that she had written for her college paper, and before that her high school paper, and she had never been asked to write a retraction.

"I can't." She paused, and he just looked at her. There was no sympathy on his face. "Jim, what I wrote was all true, and people need to know the truth."

Again, he sat quietly looking at her. His manner had changed. The man she thought she had come to know and respect would not have told her to write a retraction. "Do you like classic rock? Man, I do. I could sit and listen to it all day."

"What?"

The question came completely out of left field. It was like there was someone else in the room that he was talking to.

"Yeah, classic rock. There's this song by Norman Greenbaum called Spirit in the Sky. It's got a great sound and it's easy to sing along with."

She sat speechless starring at him.

"The thing is, just like your 'It's the end of the world' story, it's crap. You want to know when this world is going to end? For me, it ends the day I die. There ain't no spirit in the sky. When you die, it's all over, and if the world itself comes to an end after I die, I'm just not gonna care."

She slowly stood up holding on to the edge of the desk to steady herself. She couldn't bring herself to say anything.

"Okay, today's Tuesday. I'll expect the retraction on my desk no later than the end of business tomorrow. You can either work on it here or at home, wherever you're the most comfortable. If it's not on my desk by then, you're done as a journalist. Not just here-- I'll make sure you never write again."

She turned and walked toward the door, not able to believe what had just happened. She was almost out the door when he spoke again.

"If you decide not to write the retraction, that should be fine. I'm sure a girl with your good looks would have no trouble getting a job as a dancer in one of the gentleman's clubs here in town."

Paige walked to her desk in complete shock. That man back there was not the Jim Boyles she thought she knew. The one thing she did know was that she had to get out of this office. It was like one by one someone was pulling at the strings of her life and everything around her was coming apart. Paige gathered her things and left the office without saying anything to anybody.

Mike was on his first day off after his shift ended when he saw the news about the Dome of the Rock being destroyed and wondered if this had also been foretold. He pulled out his laptop, the one that had the files Alter had given him and started looking through the files. After a while he gave up. It was much easier to just type a phrase on your search bar and get all kinds of results. Alter had advised him against that kind of research for a couple of different reasons. One of those reasons was that there was no way to determine just how accurate that information was. Another more ominous reason was that your online activity was being monitored and recorded. The idea was unnerving that someone on the other end could do a search of their own for specific types of activity. Because of this, he and Alter had kept everything they did online generic so that it would keep their account from getting flagged. So he picked up his phone and called Alter to see if they could get together. Alter agreed that it would be a good idea for them to meet and go over the latest reported events. Mike said that this time he would come to Alter's home.

Mike put his shoes on and grabbed his car keys, laptop, and cellphone as he headed out the door to his car. Just as he was getting in his car, the cellphone started to ring. He looked at the caller ID. He didn't know who was on the other end, but the number looked familiar to him, so he answered.

"Hello?"

"Hi Mr. Reynolds. This is Paige Summers. Am I interrupting anything?"

After their last talk, he really didn't expect to hear from Paige Summers again.

"Not at all. What can I do for you, Ms. Summers?"

"I'm assuming you have seen the news about the Dome of the Rock. It's pretty much dominating the news cycle at the moment. There was something in the news report that caught my eye, and I would kind of like yours and your friend's opinion on the part that caught my eye."

This was definitely unexpected. He figured she had written them off as a couple of crazies the last time they had met. He also thought Alter would be okay with this change.

"Alter and I were just about to get together and go over the news report. If you remember the diner called Annie's where we first met, we could meet there if you can take a little time off work and meet us there in about an hour?"

"Yeah, I can meet you there. It seems I've got all the time in the world."

Mike ended the call and got in his car to head to Alter's apartment. He figured he would let Alter know about the call he just got, and then the two of them could head over to the diner. When he got to Alter's apartment, he let him know about the call from Paige and that she also had some questions about the latest news report. Alter took a few minutes to gather his stuff, and then the two of them got in Mike's car and headed to the diner.

Both of the men were surprised to see that, even though they were about fifteen minutes earlier than Mike had told Paige he could meet her, she was there in the diner waiting when they arrived. As soon as they walked over to her table, the waitress brought over a cup of coffee for each of them and said she would be right back with their pie. Both men had a surprised look on their faces.

"I took the liberty of ordering for you as soon as I got here. She's bringing apple pie for each of us," Paige told them with a smile. She didn't know what had made her call Mike, or for that matter what she hoped they could tell her.

Mike was the first to speak. "Ms. Summers, after our last conversation, I was sorta left with the belief that I would never hear from you again. I have to say, that I was surprised to get your call."

Here it was, she was being asked to explain something she didn't understand herself. She took a sip of her coffee and just then the waitress showed up with the slices of pie she had ordered. Paige took advantage of the moment to try to gather her thoughts. She didn't speak until she had finished her first bite of pie. "You're right. After our first talk, I thought you were a couple of crazies. Something happened today that has given me a very different perspective. I lost my job this morning because I refused to write a retraction of the story I wrote about the plague." As soon as she said it, she realized, that was the reason she had called Mike. "Now that I think about it, the story I wrote does sound crazy. Even so, the facts are all there. Nothing in that story was made up. So as crazy as your theory sounds, I'm ready to listen to you."

Mike understood. He remembered how he felt right after Alter had shared this with him. Mike had gone on his own journey of discovery before he had accepted the truth, and if he was honest with himself, there were still moments of doubt. Paige was at the beginning of a similar journey, and there was no way to tell where it would end.

Mike knew whatever he and Alter said or did at this stage would have to be slow and careful.

It was Alter who broke the silence. "Ms. Summers, I'm sorry about your job. Is there anything we can do to help?"

"No, I'm good, even though it took a little time for the initial shock to wear off. My contract has a decent separation agreement that I will be able to use. I talked to the H.R. department, and by their reaction, or lack thereof, I don't think this is the first time this has happened with people who work for Jim Boyles. The more I think about it, the more at ease I am. One thing he said, or threatened, was that age-old 'you'll never work in this town again' line. I'm embarrassed to say, it worked on me for a minute. I realize now that the man's so full of it, his eyes are brown." She laughed at her own joke and took another bite of pie. Both Mike and Alter were relieved to see how calm she was. "Now, to change the subject, I wanted to ask you about something I read in the news report. The part that got my attention was a statement made by Prime Minister Corsetti, who's the new leader of the European Union or the New World Order. It was just recently that the E.U. made the headlines when it went through a name change to

The New World Order. I didn't think much about it at the time. Frankly, I don't think anyone did, but over the last couple of hours I've pulled up some information about them. Do you remember when we met last, as I was leaving, you told me to watch the news and look for the formation of a new type of government?"

Mike, who had remembered the warning he had given her, nodded his head.

"Well, the more I look into this World Order, I can't decide if it sounds pretty cool or downright ominous."

Alter stopped eating his pie and looked at her with an expression of concern. "I would be very interested to learn what you've found out."

Paige was now on a bit of a roll and couldn't stop even if she wanted to. She took another bite of pie and a sip of coffee before continuing. Both Alter and Mike were paying very close attention to her. "I learned that for a country to join this 'Order', that country has to give up its sovereignty and fall under the leadership of the Order. So, now, there is no Prime Minister of Germany, France, Spain, or any of the countries that have joined the Order. All of these countries are under one government, and Prime Minister Corsetti is the ruler of all these nations."

Paige paused to let that sink in before she went on. "That's the potentially scary part. This next part is kinda cool and makes sense. All of these countries have gone cashless. To say cashless is a major understatement. The currency of the Order itself is now an electronic credit and their citizens have some sort of I.D. chip implanted that allows them to interact instantly anywhere in any of those countries. The chip is hacker-proof, and it carries not only your cash, but all of your information. Now for citizens of the Order there is no need for a passport, driver's license, credit card, or any kind of cash. They have truly taken cashless to an all-new level. We could use a system like that here in the U.S."

While she was talking Alter had pulled out his laptop and she could tell he was looking for something. "Let me read something to you," he said when she had finished telling them about the cashless system. "Now keep in mind this was written more than two thousand years ago. So, instead of telling you what it says, I'll just let you read it for yourself." Then he turned the laptop around for her so she could see what was on the screen. On the top of the page, it said:

'It also forced all people to receive a mark on their right hands or their foreheads, so that they could not buy or sell unless they had the mark, which is the name of the beast or the number of its name.'

She turned the laptop back towards Alter. "You have to admit what you're inferring is a bit of a stretch. I mean the system the Order has gone to is not being forced on anyone, and there is no 'mark'. It uses a microchip that is embedded that sends and receives information through either Bluetooth or satellite transmissions. Give me a sec and I'll show you."

With that, she pulled out her own laptop and opened the file she had made a couple of hours ago. She then turned her laptop around to Alter. "Here's the article I found about the monetary system, which, by the way, is not why I wanted to talk to the two of you. The thing that gets me is that all those governments subjected themselves to one man, and the changes happened faster than any governmental change in history. Who cares about how they are handling their money?"

Mike spoke while Alter was going through the article Paige had opened for him. "It seems that unless you figure out a way to control the monetary systems and bring them together, then there's no way to have a one-world government."

What Mike said did make sense, but on the other hand, the way that the cashless system was explained in the article she had pulled up for Alter to read, definitely sounded much better than anything else, if it worked the way it was explained. In the back of her mind, she did wonder what other kinds of programs were installed in the chip.

"Here ya go," Alter said, and then turned Paige's computer back around to her. "It says there that the microchip will interact with an antenna about the diameter of a human hair. The two best places for location of this antenna are either the back of your hand or your forehead."

Paige just stared at the article. She was in a state of shock. All of her research along with the information Mike and Alter had given her were overwhelming her. Right now she felt like she was treading out in the middle of the ocean and there was no land in sight no matter which way she turned her head. "What does all this mean?"

Mike could see the struggle she was going through. It was written all over her face. He prepared himself for a gut-wrenching reaction and began to tell her as gently as he knew how. "Paige, straight out is the only way I know how to say this. This means that, yes, there is a God, the Creator of all, and he has called his children home. The bad news is, we are about to go through the hardest seven years in the history of the earth. If we commit our lives to God and hold on to the truth we learn, in the end, we will see our loved ones again."

"What do you mean by the hardest seven years?" Paige couldn't see how things could get harder than what she had already gone through with the loss of her niece and then her sister. "What about my sister?" she asked with a tinge of panic in her voice.

Mike was taken way off guard. He started to ask her what she meant by that, and then he remembered her article saying that her sister couldn't go on with the loss and had committed suicide because of the loss of her daughter. Fortunately for him, Alter stepped in. "Paige, there are some questions we don't have any answers for. You are sitting here with a couple of guys who didn't answer God's call of salvation, 'cause if we had, neither one of us would be here talking to you. We would be among those who the world believes died in the plague."

She didn't respond, but it seemed that she accepted that he didn't have an answer for her.

"I will give you the notes that my friend Ben left. He was one of those called home, so I believe we can trust the results of his studies." Alter gave her another thumb drive and they all promised each other that they would continue to keep in close contact with each other. They also agreed on using this diner as a place to regularly meet again.

CHAPTER TWELVE

WITHIN the countries that had joined the Order, there were groups of people who did not agree with the way things were changing. Prime Minister Corsetti, who had become a master of molding public opinion, knew that he had to turn the public opinion against these groups. The way to do that was to make the general public afraid of the people in these groups. The easiest way to accomplish that would be to portray them as a dangerous group of people who are out for blood. To accomplish his goal Corsetti had a few directions to choose from, but for him, the choice was an easy one. He always did his best planning in solitude, so once again he took his private vehicle to his home on Lake Albano.

Marco liked his home because it afforded him two very important things, solitude and the freedom to move about. There was also the fact that its very opulence reminded him of all he had accomplished. At only fifty years old, he was one of the most powerful men on the planet, and soon he would eclipse even that.

By the time he arrived at his home, a plan had been formulated in his mind. The first thing he was going to need to do was to have Lorenzo contact a movie producer and get him to invent some news reports that will show these groups as violent terrorists. He also had to make sure that this production will be set up as a top-secret operation. The only people who could know anything about what was being done would be the ones putting on the production.

Once again Lorenzo Russo would be the main source of orchestrating the operation. No one would ever know that Marco was aware of what was being done. As soon as the production was shown to the public, he would announce investigations of these violent terrorist groups. He called Lorenzo and set up a meeting through their system of code words.

This time Lorenzo came to Marco's home for their meeting. Marco explained to his friend what he wanted to accomplish with his idea of staging terrorist attacks and blaming them on the groups that were opposing him.

"That can be arranged. However, you will likely want to eliminate all those who know how this was brought about, and being one of those in the know makes me a little nervous." Lorenzo offered with a smile.

"No, my friend you are my consigliere," he said, using the Italian word that denotes the second in command to a mob boss who serves as an adviser. "As a matter of fact, I'm about to make your position known to all. No more meeting in secret. Some things will no longer need to be a secret."

The next morning Marco awoke fresh and ready for the day. He called his driver to come and take him to the office. Today he was meeting with the president of Egypt to outline what it would mean for that country to become part of the New World Order. Marco had teams already in place to coordinate the transition. Microchips were already being mass-produced, and workers across Egypt were being trained on how to activate them and implant them into the population. After today's meeting, assimilation units would be set up throughout Egypt to facilitate the migration of the Egyptian population into the Order. After today, the president of Egypt would have a new title and new responsibilities.

Even though he was the one in control of getting everything lined up to work out the way he wanted, Marco was still surprised at how seamlessly everything had come together for him. His confidence grew stronger with every victory. The central government was becoming stronger by leaps and bounds. He promoted almost two hundred people to be leaders within the central government. Each of them was handpicked for their loyalty to him and his vision. He brought Lorenzo Russo out of the shadows and made him an official part of the new government. Lorenzo was officially head of security.

Each of the people he promoted was given the title of Praefect as well as the autonomy needed to accomplish their goal using any means they could find. Results were much quicker than they would have been under a chain of command type of bureaucracy. The title of Praefect came from ancient Roman civilization. It was a title used in the Roman empire to refer to various high ranking officials who governed territories or in some way represented Roman authority, as overseer, civil or military officer, or a tax collector.

He also met with the scientists who had developed the microchip system about initiating another phase of the system. Since everyone who had a microchip inserted was now linked to the central database, it was now time to implement the control program.

The central database could send out a signal to any identified person. This signal would cause the chip to send an electrical shock to the nervous system of the host causing instantaneous death. Only the Praefects would be told of this program. In order to let them know about the existence of the program, Marco called an assembly of the Praefects.

The assembly was held in the Roman Colosseum early the next week. Everyone was assembled on the floor of the Colosseum and there was one person there who no one recognized.

Marco walked into the middle of the group and addressed them all. "You have all been given a level of autonomy that is unprecedented," Marco said as he reached in his pocket and pulled out what looked like an electronic key fob. Then he looked at the man no one knew. "Thank you for being here. Could you tell everyone your name?"

It was obvious that the man was nervous. "Yes sir. My name is Gustaf," he said as he looked back and forth at the people in the crowd.

The Prime Minister held up the thing in his hand and pushed the button. Then with no sound, and no look of pain, Gustaf simply fell to the ground. A medic was on the scene immediately. He checked the man's vital signs and pronounced him dead. The crowd of Praefects looked on in shock while Corsetti continued to speak. "This was a demonstration of one of the capabilities built into the microchip system. I think it goes without saying that news of this capability will not go outside of this group." The subtle threat was understood by all those in the group. Everyone there knew that each of them had their own personal microchip implanted. "You are all my friends. That's why I wanted to show you the capability of this system. It's important to me that you, my friends, know all of the intricacies of the system because I am trusting you to help build an empire."

The initial outward reaction of the crowd was one of enthusiastic approval, but individually they ranged from genuine enthusiasm to fear. This was what Marco had intended and planned for. At this moment the central computer was monitoring the chemical output produced by the lymphatic system of each individual in the crowd. There were also cameras placed all around the Colosseum recording the physical reactions of each individual in the crowd. This was as close as any artificial intelligence had ever been able to come to mind reading.

One of the scientists in charge of development had jokingly called the program a beast. Marco heard about it and liked it, so he officially named the system "The Beast".

Because The Beast gave him the ability to know if someone's loyalty came more from fear than it did from belief in the vision, Marco was better equipped at choosing who was let into his inner circle. One of those he chose was a woman by the name of Deirdre Roberts, originally from Ireland. Her focus was on developing an unmanned army of sorts, an unmanned army that could carry out objectives with a limited amount of autonomy. Deirdre was told she could recruit anyone she needed from anywhere in the New World Order. One of those she recruited was an Egyptian by the name of Sabacon.

Sabacon started as a medical student at Cairo University in Egypt. He did well and was on his way to becoming an anesthesiologist. He had an almost overpowering interest in the effect different chemicals had on the human body, both physically and mentally. His career choice had been an almost natural outlet for his obsession. One day a friend asked him to go with him as he signed up for the military. He went along just to be support for his friend. When they got there, the man behind the desk mentioned that the government would reimburse him for all of his schoolings if he would sign up for a six-year commitment. He also guaranteed Sabacon that he could sign up and be an anesthesiologist with the military. It was too good to pass up, so he joined.

Once in the military, he was allowed to go into anesthesiology and he found he even had time to study his passion, the effects of different chemicals on the human nervous system. His studies got the attention of a division of the Mukhabarat, the Egyptian secret service, and he was contacted by them.

One of his subjects in particular was an experiment he was working with a chemical that in small enough doses would be non-lethal and at the same time would cause extreme pain. He discovered that just a small amount too much would cause a heart attack on a smaller animal such as a dog. He guessed that it wasn't the pain that caused the heart attack, but rather the increased heart rate, so he started adding a mild sedative with it.

The Mukhabarat wanted to have him move forward with human subjects. Sabacon was appalled when he was told about it, but they let him know that the test subjects would be prisoners who had committed some of the most hideous crimes imaginable and had been condemned to die, so he agreed.

In his opinion, the testing went well. He did lose a few subjects at first, but after only five losses he was able to achieve measurable results. One injection would last slightly more than an hour. He found out a little later that he had to wait four hours after the first injection had worn off before giving another injection. Otherwise, the subject's system couldn't handle the strain and they would die.

Another interesting side effect was that even after the effects of the first injection wore off, there was a permanent mental effect. The subject was terrified of whoever had injected them the first time. He believed that kind of side effect could be used in several ways.

CHAPTER THIRTEEN

P AIGE had spent the last two days going over the information Alter had
given her. She even followed the instructions about using the laptop.
When he gave it to her, he let her know that it was completely unable to
get online. The computer had no wifi, Bluetooth, or direct connection of
any kind. She couldn't decide if he was paranoid or so self-important that
he thought someone would be monitoring the information on the laptop.
Maybe he was a little of both. In either case, she honored his request.

Her journey over these last two days had been life-changing. Paige
was on a roller coaster of emotions. She went from overwhelming gratitude
for the sacrifice that had been made, to self-loathing because of having this
information right in front of her since she was a child and never having
paid attention to it. She couldn't forgive herself for going through her entire life so unaware. Thinking back, Paige remembered the countless times
someone had tried to talk to her and she had subconsciously shut them out.

Then she was plagued with 'what ifs'. What if she had listened back
then, she would have talked to her sister. When she thought of Amanda,
her world came crashing down again. She was hit by wave after wave of
remorse and was powerless against this onslaught of emotion. Paige begged
to be forgiven of what she considered was her willful ignorance and her
unbelief.

She wondered if it was too late to be forgiven. Then, with bitterness,
she thought if it was too late, she deserved the separation and the feeling of
being alone she felt right now.

When she could take it no longer, she called Mike. He answered
the phone on the third ring and she could hear the siren blaring in the

background letting her know he was on a run. "Could we meet when you get off?"

"Shift's over at three this afternoon. Same place?" was his answer.

"I'll be there."

The call was over.

Right at three fifteen in the afternoon, Paige pulled into the parking lot of Annie's Diner. The same waitress who had served them the first time she had met with Mike greeted her when she walked in. "Welcome back, Hun. Table for one?" The waitress had a gentle easy-going way about her which made her fit perfectly into the atmosphere of the diner.

"I've got a couple of friends who will be meeting me here."

"You want a booth or table?"

"A table would be fine."

The waitress led her to a table and Paige sat where she could see the door. She asked for a Diet Coke and said she would wait for the people joining her to order anything to eat.

She didn't have to wait long before Mike and Alter walked through the door. They saw Paige and went over to join her at the table. Both of them had brought laptops, which in the last few years people had all but stopped doing. The laptop had been replaced by the tablet or the smartphone. Paige knew that the reason for the laptops was that they had been set up to be completely blind to and from the net. When the waitress showed up, Mike and Alter both ordered a burger and fries. Realizing she hadn't eaten yet today, Paige followed their lead and ordered the same.

"Over the last two days, I've read the files you gave me a couple of times and I have some questions."

The two men looked at each other and then back at Paige then Alter spoke. "What are your questions? If we have answers we will certainly be happy to share them with you."

After their last meeting, Paige felt as if she could go straight to the heart of the reason why she needed to meet with them. "If what you told me is true, is there any hope for us, or are we done for?"

"Yes, there is hope. I'm also guessing that since you read the files and then called to talk to us, that you believe what's on them."

She paused for a few seconds before responding to Alter's assumption. When she next spoke, it was almost under her breath. "The trouble is, I do believe. The fulfillment of prophecies that are thousands of years old is undeniable. I don't see how anyone could fail to see that. I just don't understand why… why did God go to the extremes that he did?" She looked up and there were tears in her eyes. "Another question I have is, how do I know that believing makes any difference?"

Mike had been quietly listening to her and the anguish in her voice was obvious. He spoke up at her last comment. "That's where faith comes in. So many prophecies have been fulfilled, we have to trust the things that are promised that are not prophecies."

She had a quizzical look come across her face. "So, what do you mean by things that are promised?"

"Well, there are a lot of promises throughout the Bible that we can read. One that comes to mind is in Romans chapter 10 verse nine, 'If you openly declare that Jesus is Lord and believe in your heart that God raised him from the dead, you will be saved.' That's not a prophecy; that's a promise."

"Okay, I know that the prophecies are true, and from that, I know that everything else has to be true. But knowing that it's true doesn't change the way I feel. What's changed for me?"

That was the real question, what had changed for her? And she didn't know what her real question was until hearing herself asking it. Mike understood where the question came from because, in a way, he had asked that same question himself.

"What's changed for you, Paige, is your destiny. That's the promise we have."

That's when Alter spoke up. "I need to let you know that there are still things that we have to face that are going to be very hard. I believe that one day soon we will be on the run if we want to survive till the end. You also need to know that we may not survive. The Bible talks of a vast crowd of people who were martyred for not accepting the mark of the beast. Even so, it's like what Mike said, our ultimate destiny has been changed, so no matter what we have to go through, we have to remember that our destiny has been settled."

Alters' words had a chilling effect on both Mike and Paige.

"I know from what was taught in church that the period of tribulation will last for seven years, but I don't remember any specifics outside of the mark of the beast. From the studies your friend Ben had done, I'm guessing you have some information that may help us understand what's going on around us and what should we do next?"

"I've been thinking about that, and I have some ideas. We definitely should plan on meeting again, and I think we need to pay more attention to the news."

CHAPTER FOURTEEN

Then the seven angels with the seven trumpets
prepared to blow their mighty blasts.

—REVELATION 8–6

I N the months that followed their meeting, worldwide events changed
the lives of everyone on the planet. The first thing that happened was a
rolling series of hailstorms all over the planet. The description 'hailstorm'
was the closest anyone could come to vocalizing what they had witnessed.
The hail that was falling was actually on fire and caused immeasurable
damage wherever they fell. Scientists later said that the earth had come
into contact with a field of meteors that had gone virtually undetected until
coming in contact with the planet.

Countless forest fires sprang out across the globe. It seemed that nothing was out of the path of the meteor shower. Even ships on the ocean
were sunk. The loss of life was unimaginable. One of the meteors, much
larger than anything that had ever come in contact with the earth, hit in the
Pacific Ocean killing many more ocean creatures than something like that
would have. It was witnessed from miles and miles away. People who saw it
described it as a mountain that was on fire hitting the ocean.

After some investigation, it was announced that the meteor that hit in
the Pacific was radioactive. Further studies found that all the meteor showers had small amounts of radioactivity, and precautions should be taken
before eating or drinking anything.

Life itself had become a nightmare.

Mike, Paige and Alter developed a habit of meeting at Annie's, the diner they had originally met in, at least twice a week and sometimes three times in a week. The price of everything had gone up so much that even a glass of water was no longer free because so much had to be done to make it safe to drink. People now developed the habit of checking the expiration dates. The closer it was to expiration, the older it was, let people know that it had been produced before the meteor showers had hit, so it was possibly safer than those items produced after the meteor shower.

Their meetings weren't always to study prophecies or even to talk about the most recent events. Most of the time it was just to share each other's company and be a source of mutual support.

They developed the habit of praying together outside of the diner before they left going their separate directions. The prayers weren't exactly formal. They were just asking God for guidance and strength during these tough times.

Paige did get another job as a journalist despite her previous editors' threats of making sure she would never work in journalism again. It turned out that his reputation was what helped her get the job. She was told later that someone who had been blacklisted by him was always considered a good find. Her new job was slightly different than the one she had come from. She was still an investigative journalist, but now her focus was to be strictly on the assignment that had been handed to her. Before the quickening, or what the world knew as the plague, Paige would not have liked this new arrangement. In her work, she had always liked to find her own stories. Now, with all of her spare time being spent on a private subject that she couldn't share with anyone at work, her new work environment gave her the freedom for her extracurricular activities.

There had been some changes at Life Express, the ambulance service Mike and Alter worked for. To everyone's relief, they had hired a few more EMT's, and when they were brought on, Mike and Alter requested to be partnered in the same truck. It made things easier for them. Not only were they working the same shift, but since they were in the same truck, it was a guarantee that they would get off work at the same time every day.

The United States was dealt a harsh blow by the effects of the plague-the President had been flying back to D.C. that night when his plane crashed. The Vice President and his wife both died in their sleep. Under the line of succession, the office of the President fell to the Speaker of the

House of Representatives, Amy Kendrick. She became the second person in history to serve as President without being elected as President or Vice President.

Then the world was hit with radioactive meteor showers plunging the economies of the world into a tailspin. The United States government seemed to be in a state of shock.

The Soviet Union and China both saw this as an opportunity that had never happened before and likely would never happen again. Both countries quietly and quickly made preparations to take advantage of this once-in-a-lifetime opportunity. It began with an announcement of a trade agreement between the two of them. This announcement was unsettling for many other countries because the combined strength of these two giants could be world-shaking. Then both China and Russia imposed a trade embargo on the United States demanding an end to what they called the colonization efforts of the U.S. The demands of the embargo called for the closure of all military bases that were located outside of the U.S. The reactions from the rest of the globe were instant and varied. The United Kingdom, Australia, Mexico, and Brazil aligned themselves with the U.S. Argentina and India both sent ambassadors to Russia and China to sign trade agreements. Lines were quickly drawn.

President Kendrick knew that she was sitting on a powder keg with the fuse lit. She had spent the last twenty years working in both state and federal governments and she had never seen events like this. Historically, tensions like this never happened so quickly. What used to take years to develop was now happening in days. It was like riding a roller coaster without the slow climb up the hill. As soon as you got in the car, you were gone, with no time to prepare or even think about it.

She met with her cabinet and laid out the demands of the embargo, then opened the meeting for discussion. The Treasury Secretary was the first to speak. "I think the embargo will likely hurt them as much or more than it hurts us, so we could just let it play out. See who blinks first."

"What if we comply? I mean, let's look at it logically. With everything that's happened, we are stretched way too thin as it is. It would likely help us to move our military out of those bases and bring them back home." That was from the Secretary of Interior.

With that President Kendrick said, "If we comply, it would be the same as giving in to the demands of a terrorist. We have never done that in the history of this country, and I'll be dammed if I let it happen on my watch."

The discussion went back and forth for several minutes until the Secretary of Defense spoke. General Brian Ash was a retired three-star general who had been appointed to this job two years ago. "There is one option that you've all been avoiding since this meeting began. That is to employ our Preemptive policy that we have had in place since two thousand and one." Everyone in the room quietly focused their attention on the retired Army General. Seeing that he had everyone's attention, Ash continued. "We already have assault plans on both China and Russia. Those contingencies have been around for years. Hell, most of our military exercises are based on those plans."

When he said that someone asked the question. "Are you suggesting that we declare war on China and Russia?"

With that, Ash shook his head and chuckled softly. "What I'm saying is that the best way to avoid a long bloody war is to strike a decisive blow while everyone else is posturing. A schoolyard bully gets his way by threats and picking on people who don't fight back, but the second some kid knocks him on his ass when he's least expecting it, he backs off."

At that, President Kendrick spoke up. "That sounds good on the surface General, but this isn't a schoolyard, and if we do what you are suggesting, people are going to die, and they will die because I gave the order."

"Yes, Madam President, we will have losses, but with all due respect, that is why our guys signed up, to fight for the American cause."

At the same time, across the globe, Marco Corsetti was in a meeting he had called with his team leaders to discuss how the New World Order would respond to this conflict between the other world powers. The general consensus with all of them was that it would be best for the Order to remain neutral and let these heavyweights fight it out between themselves. Prime Minister Corsetti agreed and ordered that a statement of Neutrality be put forth. His next step would be to arrange a teleconference with Ben Aaron of Israel before the statement of Neutrality was published and speak to him of the wisdom in remaining neutral as well.

Mike called Alter who had been watching the news report himself. They both agreed that the three of them needed to meet right away. Mike hung up, called Paige back to let her know, then he grabbed his laptop and headed out the door.

Within the hour, Prime Minister Corsetti was on a conference call with Ben Aaron, the Prime Minister of Israel, and his closest advisers. Corsetti told Aaron of the statement that was about to be released to the world stating that The New World Order would maintain complete neutrality during this conflict. The statement also said that he looked forward to the time when this world would finally know peace. Ben Aaron assured Corsetti that Israel would not get involved. His country had seen conflict for so many years that the people of Israel wanted desperately to live in peace. Marco believed that and knew he did not need to persuade Prime Minister Aaron to stay away from the conflict. He continued the call but changed the subject. "That is a very wise decision my friend, and since I have you on the line, I would like to extend an offer I had made in passing during our meeting in Rome." He paused briefly and then started to speak again. "Since the Caliph announced that they would not rebuild their Mosque in Jerusalem, I would like to offer my engineers and laborers along with the necessary material to finally build a new temple on that historic site."

Corsetti explained that what he was offering was simply a very small token of reparations for what his Roman ancestors had done to the Jewish people. After a few minutes of conversation, Prime Minister Aaron accepted the offer and agreed on a day for the engineers of the Order to visit the site and begin the process of building the temple.

Mike, Paige, and Alter all pulled into the parking lot of the diner at the same time. The hostess recognized them as they were walking in and led them to a table. As they were sitting down, she let them know that their coffee was on the way and a waitress would come by in a sec to take their order.

"It didn't take them long to get used to us, did it?" Alter asked. Then before anyone said anything in response to his comment, the waitress was there with their coffee, ready to take their order. Paige ordered two eggs over easy with bacon while the two guys ordered short stacks each.

Then Paige said, "We keep meeting here and I'm gonna gain some unwanted pounds."

"I doubt it, not if your energy level is anything like my daughter's was. She could eat as much as she liked and never worry about gaining weight." Mike said, and then suddenly looked down at the table. When he looked up again, he had to wipe tears from his eyes. "I'm sorry," he said. "It's just that I miss my girls so much."

Then in an effort to gain control of his emotions he turned his attention to Alter. "Well, I'm pretty sure this is not the beginning of the battle of Armageddon, so what exactly is this?"

Alter took a sip of his coffee as the waitress brought their order to the table. As soon as she was gone, Alter took a bite and said what he thought this latest event could mean. "The prophecies do mention a war before the battle of Armageddon, and it would make sense for the world to go through something catastrophic before any kind of world leader would be accepted. I guess that we need to pay attention and notice whoever negotiates peace. That person will be our ultimate enemy."

He put his laptop on the table, turned it on, and opened a file. Once he found what he was looking for he moved around so they could all see the screen at the same time. "This is it right here," he said, pointing to the screen. The open file was the downloaded bible program. He had Revelation chapter nine brought up. "Here starting in verse fourteen it talks about four angels who are turned loose to kill one-third of the population of the earth with an army of over two hundred million."

Then he clicked on another file. "In his notes, Ben names several theologians who believed that the four angels mentioned here are a world war. What's happening now lines up with that interpretation. The U.S. has never had an embargo of any kind placed on them. Based on the prophecies, I do believe that war is inevitable."

Mike spoke next and there was a distinct sadness in his voice. "In my whole life, I never expected to be faced with the possibility of war."

Paige could hear the pain in Mike's voice. It was a pain and sadness she also felt. Then she had a jolt of fear hit her consciousness. "Do you think this will become a nuclear war?"

Alter answered her the best he knew how. "I think it's possible. A nuclear strike would be one way for a third of the population of the earth to be killed. Whether or not this becomes a nuclear war, I can't imagine how catastrophic it's going to be. We're talking about over a billion people being wiped out. The prophecy even goes on to say that unless God shortens the period, that no one on earth will survive. We are going to have to face the possibility that one of us or all of us will not survive this war."

CHAPTER FIFTEEN

T HE plan was to deliver crippling attacks on both Russia and China. If successful, these attacks would eliminate their nuclear strike capabilities. Russia had over fifteen hundred land-based nuclear missiles plus an additional three hundred ICBM's in submarines located all over the world. China's known arsenal was a fraction of that, with only three hundred warheads total. The plan was on the surface a simple one. Destroy the command centers in Russia and their communication hubs while simultaneously launching a strike on the nuclear weapons R&D center in China. With the communications knocked out in Russia, U.S. forces would be able to advance with minimal casualties. Then with both countries unable to mount a strong response, the U.S. and their allies would be able to enforce their will.

President Kendrick gave her generals the flexibility to come up with a workable plan that could be put into action immediately. Within hours of her giving the go-ahead, several teams of strategists were assembled going over every possible way the plan could go wrong and eliminating the possible flaws in the plans. In the end, they came up with an altered version of Operation Dropshot. This was the code name for a military operation that had originally been devised at the end of World War II and then officially taken off the books in nineteen seventy-seven. Unofficially over the years, Dropshot was still an ever-evolving plan that had evolved to include the existence of Russian ICBM's and satellite communications that did not exist when the plan was originally conceived.

With every possible contingency accounted for, the go order was given, and the operation was put into motion.

The strike in China was to be carried out by a flight of eight B-2 bombers, each one loaded with eighty quarter ton bombs. These were stealth bombers designed for penetrating dense anti-aircraft defenses. They were spread out over several hundred miles of airspace and each one was flanked by a pair of F-22 Raptors. The Raptor was designed primarily as an air superiority fighter. It also had ground attack as well as electronic warfare capabilities.

The strike was launched from the U.S. airbase in the province area of Pampanga in the Philippines.

The strike in Russia was launched out of Fort Richardson Army base out of Anchorage Alaska. This was a joint strike using both the Army and the Air Force.

The operation into Russia was the one most likely to run into a problem because there were multiple points of attack using a combination of ground forces and airstrikes. There was also an ultra high altitude aspect to the attack. For this part of the operation, the decision was to use the A-72 Lightning Strike.

The A-72 Lightning Strike could have been called the grandchild of the SR-71 Blackbird, which had been decommissioned in the late nineties. First came the SR-72, which was the next generation of the Blackbird. One look at it, and anyone could see the resemblance. It had an aggressively sloped body, molding itself into the wings. Rather than having its twin engines on the wings, the twins of the 72 were part of the fuselage. It had a ceiling of over 90,000 feet and a max speed in excess of Mach 6, or six times the speed of sound. It was, by all intents and purposes, a spacecraft without having to dump a solid-fuel rocket after takeoff. This enabled it to go on an unlimited number of missions.

Then someone at Lockheed came up with the idea of building a prototype that would be able to carry weapons instead of surveillance equipment, and from that idea came the A-72. The difference in the names was that SR meant surveillance and reconnaissance for the SR-72 and the A-72 stood for an attack aircraft.

The weapons payload for the A-72 was just as unconventional as the plane itself. Since the max speed of current hypersonic missiles was around Mach 5 and the A-72 could maintain a speed of Mach 6. The decision was made to equip the plane with a directed energy weapon, or DEW. The DEW was a medium-range weapon that damages its target with highly focused energy, including laser, microwaves, and particle beams. The engineers considered the DEW to be the obvious choice for such a futuristic attack plane and dubbed the new weapon the A-72 Lightning Strike.

The Lightning Strike, as well as the updated Blackbird, were both put into operation secretly. They only flew out of specific airfields, but with their long-range capabilities, there wasn't any place on the globe they could not strike. The flight crews, pilots, and anyone who was even slightly connected with the birds were given detailed assignments as cover stories. All of them had to pass a top-secret security clearance protocol. These birds were the best-kept secret of the Air Force.

The plan was to use thirty of these birds to take out the satellite communications of Russia, making them unable to communicate with any of their nuclear-armed subs. Because Russia had such a large number of communications satellites in orbit, the 72's were going to have to take out multiple satellites each, making their long-range and speed critical to the mission. With their communications taken out, no strike orders could be given to the nuclear-capable subs.

Both strikes were given the "go" order, and so it began.

Within hours of the order being given, bombs began to hit China, and for the first time in history, the U.S. had initiated the first strike. The war had begun.

In recent history, the country that made the first strike in a war never achieved its true goal, no matter how devastating that first strike was. The United States was the recipient of two such strikes. The first was December 7th, 1941, the attack on Pearl Harbor. The second was September 11th, 2001, the attack on the Twin Towers. In both cases, America did recover and then struck a blow that devastated their attackers.

Perhaps America's newest president, Amy Kendrick, failed to consider what would happen if the roles in both of those scenarios had been reversed.

Even though the air attack on China was devastating, the attacks on Russia did not go as well as they had been planned. The first problem came from the ground assault. Russia had detected the movements of the forces, and in turn, mobilized their forces. Although this had been expected by the U.S., the one thing that had been unexpected was the sheer numbers Russia was prepared with. Both sides suffered heavy losses, but the U. S. and her allies were unable to destroy the communications hub.

The A-72 Lightning Strikes, however, did exactly what the plan had called for. These highly trained pilots, commanded by Major Skip Williams, call sign, Perseus, carried out their objective flawlessly. They eliminated every Russian communication satellite. Each pilot had been given his objective pre-launch along with the autonomy to carry it out with no communication needed once he had taken off. It wasn't designed to be a controlled attack, so there would be no transmissions that could be intercepted once the mission was underway.

Because of its stealth design, Mach-6 speed, extremely high altitude, and the use of the DEW, the A-72's silently destroyed every one of the satellites.

There was one thing that the U.S. didn't know about, and that was that Russia and China had developed a line of communication that was separate from their current lines. It wasn't because they anticipated an attack, but because they didn't want any communications intercepted. There was no central hub for the network so if one station were incapacitated the rest of the network would continue to function as if nothing had happened, and it wasn't satellite-based.

The attacks launched by the U.S. were successful with their assignments. In one day, China's nuclear capabilities, as well as Russia's launch communications, were completely taken out. The flaw was that the U.S. had no intelligence on the communication network that was being used by Russia and China. Because it was unknown by the Americans and subsequently left alone, news of the attack was sent down the line. The communications network was being monitored by one of the Borei class submarines of Russia. At the time of the attack, the sub was in the Atlantic Ocean, approximately three thousand miles off the coast of North America.

The primary purpose of Borei-class submarines was almost unimaginably grim: to bring ruin to an adversary's cities, even should other nuclear forces be wiped out in a first strike. One Borei can rain seventy-two nuclear warheads, each ten times more destructive than the bomb dropped on Hiroshima. The existence and purpose of this class of submarines were known by the U.S. government. One problem was that the exact location of the sub was never really known. That was why the object of the strike was to disable all communications and in doing so, cripple Russia with the one strike.

When communications over the wire talked about a devastating attack on China and at the same time all communications with Russia were down, the commander of the sub concluded that the attack was from the Americans. Any other sub commander would not have acted without an order, especially since there was nothing concrete saying that the attack had come from America. This commander did something completely against all of his training. He launched missiles towards the United States.

Even though the U.S. didn't account for the communications network existing, they did have a contingency plan in case something went wrong with the strike. The contingency was to be prepared for an immediate counter strike.

All but one of the missiles were intercepted by the long-established missile defense network. That one missile impacted the northeastern shore of the United States, killing millions.

President Kendrick had survived the initial attack of the Russian submarines because before the initial strikes on Russia and China she and the cabinet had been shuttled into elaborate bomb shelters designed specifically for the President and the President's staff. The facility was the Raven Rock Mountain Complex in Pennsylvania. Also known as Site R, it was a U.S. military installation with an underground nuclear bunker near Blue Ridge Summit, Pennsylvania, at Raven Rock Mountain. It had been called the "Underground Pentagon". The bunker had emergency operations centers for the United States Army, Navy, and Air Force. Along with Mount Weather Emergency Operations Center in Virginia and the Cheyenne Mountain Complex in Colorado, it formed the core bunker complexes designed to survive a nuclear attack.

"What just happened?" She wasn't asking anyone in particular. It was just an uncontrolled response. Everyone around her understood that she knew what had just happened so no one said anything.

"Ma'am, we will be getting reports any minute now on how damaging the strike was."

She couldn't believe this was happening. She had become the President because of a worldwide tragedy and now after being President for a little more than a year, she had become one of the instigating factors of a nuclear war.

What resulted was a horror beyond imagination. In that one strike, the United States lost close to three million people. When the U.S. retaliated it was immediate, and almost in the way a wounded snake would strike at anything that moves, the U.S. launched nuclear warheads at both Russia and China killing hundreds of millions. Never in the history of the globe had anything like this ever happened. News reports declared the beginning of World War Three had begun and many believed that this would be the end of the human race.

The first objective of every country was to try and disable their opponent's nuclear capability. Since nuclear weapons had already been used, the fear was that they would escalate into a worldwide holocaust wiping out the global population.

Almost a week had passed since Mike, Paige and Alter had last met at the diner. The people of America were in a state of shock. Nothing like this had ever been imagined. Mike and Alter had just finished their second night of the third shift. Mike's phone started ringing as he was opening the door to his house. He looked at the caller I.D. and saw that it was Paige calling him. He answered the phone as he was walking inside. "Hi Paige, are you OK?"

"What are we supposed to do?" she asked. "Is this the beginning of the war that Alter's friend talked about? I thought it was going to have something to do with Israel, not Russia and China."

"I don't know. Let me call Alter and see if we can meet at the diner to talk about it."

"OK when?"

"Right now, as far as I'm concerned. I'll call you back as soon as I talk to Alter."

Chapter Sixteen

With all of the major powers of the world-destroying each other, Marco Corsetti secretly sent ambassadors to the U.S., England, Russia, and China. Even though there were other countries involved, these four were the pendulum on which this war swung. Each ambassador carried a message saying that the New World Order wanted to ally itself with that country. The ambassadors delivered an invitation to the leaders of each country to come to Rome for negotiations of allegiance. The date and location were agreed by the leaders of every nation. None of them were aware that the others had been invited to the same place on the same date.

The dignitaries were each scheduled to arrive unknowingly on a timed schedule with two hours between arrivals. The meetings were supposed to be private and intimate, so each leader was asked to leave their security detail outside of the office, and Prime Minister Corsetti would have his personal assistant escort them into the meeting. Again, the arrival times of the leaders were spaced far enough apart to allow teams that were hired by Lorenzo Russo to quietly subdue each security detail and remove them before the next world leader arrived.

Upon walking through the door, each world leader was met by a small team who forced them to sit down at a conference table. Then with no fanfare, Marco Corsetti walked into the room. As he walked in, each of the world leaders felt a heavy hand being placed on their shoulder to keep them still and quiet.

"Gentlemen," he glanced at Amy Kendrick, "and Madam." His tone and demeanor were eerily calm. Judging by the way he presented himself, no one would believe that he had just orchestrated the capture of the leaders of the four most powerful countries in the world. "I apologize for the subterfuge that it took to get you all here today, but I promise you that when this is finished, you will see that the ends do justify the means. Before this day is over, we are going to establish peace." Having said that, he took a seat at the head of the conference table. The Russian president immediately tried to get up to leave, but he was put back in his chair by the two men behind him at either side.

Marco, along with everyone else at the table, saw the attempt to leave. "Unlike the chaos all of you have created in the world, this meeting will be in order, and we will reach positive results." His manner was so calm that it was unnerving to the other world leaders. "I know that individually none of you are monsters, and that you all want the best for your people, and because I know that, I have invited you to this meeting. I know, for example, that President Kendrick mourns the loss of millions of Americans. In the same way, so do Prime Minister Vasiliev from Russia and President Ling in China. All of your countries combined have lost at or more than a billion people. All of you know that if this war isn't stopped, it will escalate to a point that the entire population of the world will be at risk. So as of today, you are all going to let your people know that you are now at peace."

Out of all the people sitting at the table, surprisingly, it was President Kendrick who spoke first.

"Prime Minister Corsetti, first of all, congratulations on your accomplishments to date. This, however, is not one of those accomplishments. As we sit here, a U.S. strike team has gotten into place and is about to move in with devastating speed and force. You have attempted the kidnapping of a sitting U.S. President. No one on this planet is so deceived to believe that they could get away with something like that."

The other leaders nodded their heads in partial agreement with what President Kendrick had just said.

Marco seemed unaffected by what she had just said. He just smiled and with a manner of an adult patiently correcting a child said, "Please, all of you listen closely to what I'm about to say. That way it need not be repeated again and again." He stood from his chair and began to pace slowly back and forth. He resembled a college professor lecturing his class. "There are operatives placed at high levels in each of your governments. We intimately know the details of the security measures of all of your countries. Let me assure you that no one is coming. I know that most of you don't believe me. I also know that all of your security measures have a response time of less than an hour if calls aren't received to let them know that all is well. So, to prove to you all that what I say is true, I'm going to leave you here and I'll be back in two hours. While I'm gone, each of you will be given a receiver that can monitor all of your government frequencies. That way, you will know that no emergency messages are being transmitted."

Then at his signal, receivers were placed in front of each of the people sitting at the table. With no further comment, Marco Corsetti quietly got up and left the room.

Mike Paige and Alter all pulled into the diner at almost the same time. The atmosphere of the diner was somber as the three of them sat at their table. It wasn't just Mike, Alter, and Paige who were in a state of confused shock. It was everyone, everywhere. Almost the entire east coast had been declared a disaster area because of the blast area and the nuclear fallout zone. The number of dead and dying were unimaginable. Some people were going through their normal routines, but it was obvious that they were just running on autopilot because they didn't know what else to do with their life. It had been almost a year since the worldwide plague hit, and since that day, the events across the globe had happened so fast that it didn't feel like there was a moment to at least take a breath before something else horrible happened.

"I'm not sure I can take much more of this," Paige said.

Alter put his hand on her shoulder. "This is hard on all of us."

Then Mike added, "But we are at least here for each other, even when things get worse."

At that, Paige looked at him with a troubled look on her face. "Things are going to get worse? A nuclear warhead just hit this country on the east coast and probably killed millions. Before that, there was the meteor shower that killed people all over the globe. Our economy has completely spiraled out of control. Then, of course, there was the plague that started us down this road in the first place. Now you tell me that things are going to get worse. Why doesn't God just blow up the planet and be done with it?"

"Paige." Alter said her name in a way that caught her attention. "You know that all of this was our fault, I mean, mankind's fault. And yes, it is going to get worse, much worse. The prophecies say that unless God shortens the days of this tribulation that no one on earth would survive. That's why we need to plan our getaway."

Hearing Alter say that in such a matter-of-fact way disturbed Paige deep in her core. Yet at the same time, something within her said that Alter was right. She looked down at the yet untouched omelet in front of her, and despite her earlier hunger, felt a wave of nausea. She pushed it further away from her.

"Escape to where? I mean, as far as I can tell, there's not a safe place anywhere on Earth we can go," Mike asked.

With that question, Alter hesitated, then looked at them both and said, "Most interpretations of the prophecies speak of two places. One is a vague reference to a wilderness, and they give no specifics as to where. Someplace in a wilderness does make sense, because I think our biggest threat in the near future will come from people around us."

"What about the other place?" Paige asked. "I mean, you said it yourself, this wilderness location sounds vague."

"The other location is in Jordan. It's called Petra."

Mike spoke up. "You're talking about the other side of the world, and from what I understand, that's one place we don't want to be when everything comes to a head."

Paige was confused. "What are you two talking about?"

Mike gestured towards Alter. "He's saying that we should go camp out practically right next to the site of the Battle of Armageddon."

With a concerned look on her face, Paige asked, "Isn't that the battle you two said was going to happen at the end of the seven years?"

Alter was unmoved by Mikes' comments. "The Bible talks about a woman running from a dragon, and the wilderness hiding her from the dragon. Most scholars agreed that the woman the scripture talked about will be those who come to believe after the rapture. Obviously, the dragon is Satan and the people he owns. Things will deteriorate very fast in the days to come. I think that people like us will be considered outlaws, and those who you would consider friends will turn you over to the government. We may not survive until the end. If we do get caught, we have to hold on to the truth we have learned. In the end, it's that truth that will save us."

Mike put his coffee down and with a look of resignation he asked, "So what do you propose we do now?"

With that question, Alter shook his head and shrugged his shoulders. "I don't know exactly. I feel like we should figure out a way to get over there in a way that is as secret as we can make it."

"I may have an idea," Paige said, and both Alter and Mike looked at her in surprise. "Don't look so surprised, I do get ideas every now and then."

"I'm just surprised at how quickly you adapt to situations. What's your idea?"

Without waiting for Mike to respond Paige spoke up. "A couple of years ago I did a story about cartels smuggling drugs using shipping containers on cargo ships. I got to know one of the captains of a cargo ship. He was one of the people I contacted when the warhead hit the east coast. Fortunately for him, his ship was off the coast of Africa when it hit, so he and his crew survived. He said that he is moving his base port to Miami. That way he can maintain his operations and stay away from the fallout zone. I can get in touch with him and say I'm wanting to do a story on the effect the blast has had on the shipping industry, tell him I plan to go on a run with him on his next trip to Africa. The two of you could be my research assistants. That would at least give us passage to that part of the world."

No one said anything at first. Then, after a pause, Alter was the first who spoke. "We need to sell everything we can and take as much cash with us as possible."

"My car's paid for. I could sell it fairly quickly." Mike added.

Alter listed a few things he had that could sell quickly enough and Paige mentioned that she had a savings account that she could empty. The three of them sat there in the diner and put together a getaway plan and then they agreed to put it into motion right away while they still could move around the country without causing any real suspicion. According to the interpretation that Alter's friend had left, their ability to move around freely would not last much longer. Alter also warned them that the attitude of the people around them would very quickly begin to change to where those who they would consider friends would believe it a good thing to turn any of the three of them over to the authorities. Paige thought about how her former editor had turned on her so viciously that last day in his office. With that memory fresh in her mind, she did not doubt that Alter's warning was right on target, and there was no one they could trust. They agreed to act as quickly as they could. When they left the diner, Alter agreed to follow Mike to his house so he could get his car title and take his car to a dealership that offered cash on the spot for cars. Paige went to her bank and emptied her savings. They also decided to use their credit cards for anything in the states and then switch to cash once they were overseas.

The plan was to use Paige's idea of pretending to write a story on the shipping industry. They would use that story to be able to get on a cargo ship headed to Africa and once there, they would use overland transportation to make their trek across to Jordan.

Then later that afternoon a breaking news story gave them a real sense of urgency.

After Mike sold his car, Alter gave him a ride home. Not wanting to look suspicious, they decided it would be best for them to go ahead and show up at work. Paige would call them as soon as she talked to the ship's captain. Then the three of them would begin their journey. They set a time the next day for Alter to pick Mike up and give him a ride to work then there was a knock on the door.

Mike opened the door to see Paige standing there holding a newspaper with a look on her face that, because of the nature of his job, was all too familiar. Paige had the shocked expression of someone who had just witnessed a devastating event.

"Have you seen the news?" she asked, almost shoving the paper in his face. The article she was referring to was on the front page.

End of the War

A pact between all of the governments of the world has been reached. The leaders of the countries who have been part of this war just came out of a top-secret meeting where they have agreed to end hostilities. The instigator of this meeting was Marco Corsetti, the director of the New World Order. He has released a statement which we will make available to the public with no delay. It gives his reasons and upcoming plans. One quote from that statement is as follows:

"The citizens of the world want and deserve peace. This war, in its infancy, has already claimed the lives of almost a billion people. If the war is allowed to continue, it will create what is known as nuclear winter and no one will survive. It has to be stopped right now."

The details of the pact are soon going to be released, and when they are, this paper will make every detail available. There have been several studies on what would happen if America and Russia were to engage in a nuclear war and we have seen a small taste of that, a very small taste. Some are asking what the cost of this peace is, but for the millions who have just lost a loved one, peace and security are worth any price. Today will be spoken of in history as the day the world found peace."

The article went on to explain that this announcement was being made in countries all over the world and this day would become a worldwide day of celebration from now on.

The three of them sat in silence for a few minutes, each of them lost in their thoughts. Mike finally broke the silence. "There's probably not a better time than right now for us to put our escape plan in motion."

"You're right," Alter answered.

"This is likely the best window of opportunity we have."

Then when what all three of them had been had thinking had been spoken, they all just sat there looking at each other. Planning something like this and putting it into motion were two very different things. Each of them knew that as soon as the first step was taken, there would be no turning back.

For Mike, this journey had begun when he realized that his wife and daughter had been caught up and he had been left behind. At first his commitment came from his desire to be reunited with them, and even though that was still a strong desire, his commitment to the Father was now even stronger.

Paige, who had rejected even the thought of God all her life, had turned to him unreservedly when the truth slapped her in the face. Although she knew there was still so much to learn, she considered herself all in.

Alter felt as if he had been on the cusp of accepting the truth before, and now that he knew the truth, he truly didn't care what the cost was to follow the truth.

So even before any of them said a word to each other, they had all committed.

Paige was the first to speak. "Our first stop has to be my house. I've got the contact information for the ship's captain there. I'll call him and let him know I would like to do a story on the effect the war had on the shipping industry. I'll let him know I'm on the way with a small crew."

Then without any further conversation, they left Mike's house together, never to return.

CHAPTER SEVENTEEN

THINGS were moving along very much the way Marco had planned. The heads of each of the countries that had been involved in the war were now implanted with the microchip. Each of them had also assured the Prime Minister that their country would cooperate in the effort of world-wide peace. Either willingly or unwillingly, each of them pledged that their country would give up their sovereignty and join the New World Order. Because they pledged loyalty and support, each head of State was offered a position of prominence in the Order. They would then, in turn, go back home to their country and begin the transition. Each of them was assured that Prime Minister Corsetti had thousands of engineers and technicians, whose job it would be to facilitate the new worldwide monetary system.

At the same time, there were teams in Israel working with the Jewish Rabbis to rebuild Solomon's temple on the spot where the Dome of the Rock had once stood. The efficiency of all his plans working together like they were doing was truly amazing. No one in the history of the world had ever been able to accomplish so much in so little time. He had been able to do all of this without declaring war. Not even the ancient Roman Empire had been able to gain the peaceful cooperation of its subjects, and while the Roman Empire had ruled an incredible amount of countries and territories, the New World Order now ruled the planet.

There was no logical way for any of this to happen, yet here it was. The world was now finally at peace.

Mike, Paige, and Alter listened to the news on the car radio as they were driving to Miami, on their way to meet the ship's captain.

The announcement was made by the current President of the United States. Even though this was an expected announcement, it was still unsettling to witness foretold events happening right in front of you.

"My fellow citizens, this is a time of celebration. For the first time in the history of the world, we now have peace across the globe. Not only do we have peace, but measures have also been put into place to ensure this peace will last for generations to come. We are now all part of The New World Order with Minister Corsetti at the helm of our ship. This is an exciting time of change, not just for us, but for the entire planet. As I speak, teams are being sent all over the globe to help facilitate the transition into the new system. Because of this new system, borders across the globe will disappear. You will no longer need a passport to travel anywhere on the planet. There will no longer be a need to exchange your currency from one country to another. The price of goods across the planet will stabilize. A loaf of bread will cost the same here as it does in China. Countries will no longer have to designate huge amounts of resources to build up their military. Those resources can now be diverted into programs that help the citizens of the world. This truly is an exciting time to be alive. A transition center will soon be set up near where you live, and you will be notified as to when you are to report to the center to complete your transition. Minister Corsetti is scheduled to deliver an address tomorrow evening, and soon afterward the transition teams will begin to reach out to you."

Marco Corsetti turned off the feed he had been watching. The United States was the second of several scheduled announcements that would run today. It was hard to believe, but everything seemed to be working out just the way he had planned. Except for some small insignificant places, he, Marco Corsetti, was now the ruler of the planet. As of today, he had surpassed both Attila the Hun and Genghis Khan. He had achieved what they had only dreamed of and without a single battle. He knew there would be pockets of resistance to the changes, but he was confident that the resistance could be dealt with quickly without disturbing his plan. His strongest weapon would be the ability to control public opinion. The way to control public opinion was easy, just control the information the public received. A truly free press was the enemy of progress as was a press that was openly controlled by the government.

With that in mind, those who controlled the press all over the world would be the first to be brought into the centers for the transition. Then, after the chip was implanted, they would be privately informed of the abilities this system had. The system was affectionately called the Beast, because of its size and ability to track and monitor everyone on the globe. There was also the ability to eliminate a single person or an entire group with one command. They had to know that the chip would completely integrate itself with their nervous system so that any attempt to remove it would be fatal.

In a small amount of time, the Beast would have control over most of the people on the planet, and Corsetti would be in control of the Beast.

Mike, Paige, and Alter sat in stunned silence after hearing the announcement on the radio. They were in Paige's car headed toward Miami. Knowing something is going to happen doesn't remove the shock you feel when you see it happen. This was the case with the three of them. They were witnessing the death of their country, and what made it worse was that most people had no idea that's what had just happened.

"So how do you think this is going to affect our plan?" Paige asked.

"I don't think it changes what we are going to do," Alter answered.

"What do you think these transition centers are going to be?" Mike asked.

Alter looked over at him and said, "The prophecies say that when the antichrist assumes control that there's going to be a mark, and that no one will be able to buy or sell without this mark."

"I've heard people talk about this before, the mark of the beast. It's hard to believe that no one is going to buy anything from you or sell anything to you unless you have six six six tattooed across your forehead," said Mike.

"The fulfillment of the prophecies is not subject to our interpretation of them. The coming of Yeshua was nothing like what we Jews thought it would have been, but looking back at it now, we can see that every prophecy about him was fulfilled. Also, the taking away of God's people- none of the studies that I've read mention anything like a plague, but looking back on it, we can see the truth of what happened. It seems that the fulfillment of a prophecy is difficult to recognize if it's happening right in front of you instead of when you are looking at it through the lens of history."

Paige wasn't following the conversation as well as she would like to. "I'm not sure what all that means," she said.

So, Alter answered her, "What I mean is, that I don't know what the mark of the beast that's talked about in the Bible is going to be. I do believe it will be linked to a global economy that will make every currency now in use on the planet obsolete."

Hearing that frustrated Paige. "Then what are we doing with all this cash if it won't be any good to us?"

Mike answered before Alter said anything. "We will be able to use our cash during the transition period, and there's no way that will happen overnight. Even with as fast as everything is happening now, we should have time to make it to Jordan."

"Yes, and once we get there, I'm hoping we will be able to go into hiding and live off the land," Alter finished Mike's sentence. All three of them knew it was a shaky plan, but none of them wanted to sit in Atlanta and wait to see what would happen next. They had agreed that if you wanted to get away, the best time to do that was when no one was chasing you.

They got to Miami late that night and pulled into a hotel where they could crash for the night. According to the ship's schedule, they still had another day before it left the dock. All three of them were curious to find out what time the announcement by Minister Corsetti would be. Despite their own feeling of foreboding, they wanted to hear what news this announcement was going to bring.

"My fellow citizens of The New World Order:"

Just the way the announcement started was unnerving. Watching from the hotel room in Miami, it was as if that calm smiling face had just said "I own you; your lives are now under my control."

"Today is a bright new day for the planet. For the first time in history, our world is now at peace. Before I go any further, I would like to mention my thanks to the former Russian and U.S. presidents and the efforts both of them have made in bringing this peace into being. Both of them have been very helpful in this new beginning. They have also both accepted positions on my board of advisers. It is an honor to be able to work with both of them. They have been instrumental in helping to bring about this peace.

One question you may have is what this peace means to you. And for many of you, it will mean no real change in your day-to-day lives. You'll still get up every day and go to work to take care of your families. The big change will be that you will no longer have to worry about a nuclear missile cruising toward your country bringing death for you and your family. The death toll for the war that just ended is estimated to be close to a billion people. The vast majority of the people who were killed had done nothing to deserve what happened to them. We can no longer accept that kind of risk to the people of this world. That is why the leaders of this world have agreed that they needed to join together in this mission of peace.

In order for our world to truly come together as one people, borders between people have to be erased- both physical borders and mental borders. To reach this goal, we are implementing a new system that is already active in several regions of the Order. Every person will individually be logged into the system. Once you are logged in you will officially be a citizen of the Order and be given all the privileges that go with citizenship.

Now I know that many of you are curious as to how this transition is going to happen and what the potential changes to your day-to-day life will be.

First, let me assure you that your day-to-day life is about to become less complicated. Agencies are in place and working very hard to make this transition an almost seamless process. Once you are integrated into the system, there will be no need for identification paperwork like a driver's license or any other kind of I.D. card. All of that information will be in the system. Also, because your banking and credit information will be in the system, you will have no need for cash, checks, or credit cards. All of these will become obsolete.

Once you are part of the system, identity theft will be impossible, along with any other kind of theft. Your personal security will be magnified immensely. The world is about to become a much less complicated place to live.

Transition centers are being put into operation all over the globe this week. There will be one near you wherever you are. They will reach out to each of you shortly. As soon as you are contacted, simply go report to the transition center and everything will be taken care of very quickly right there, along with answering any questions you may have."

The announcement continued with Minister Corsetti making a point to individually thank leaders from several different countries for their efforts in helping this come about.

Paige turned the TV off, and the three of them sat in the hotel room saying nothing for what felt like an eternity but was probably no more than a minute. Then Alter spoke, "My guess is, we will have some time before some of those transition centers are set up in Atlanta, and even after that, it will likely be a while before a notice is sent out for any of us. We may already be in hiding by then."

Mike was the next one to speak. "I think we should find that hiding place as quickly as possible."

"You seem like something is bothering you. Other than the whole world turning upside down, what's on your mind?" Paige asked.

"It just seems to me that time has been sped up. Things that you think would take years to develop now happen in days. I'm afraid that the same is going to be true with this whole process of converting things to the New World Order. I mean, this whole war began, killed up to a billion people, and then ended all in a matter of days."

Paige was a bit confused by what Mike had just said. "I'm not sure what you mean by that," she said.

"What I mean is that we may not have as much time as we think. Things seem to be developing unnaturally fast. I mean, who knows, if we are not part of this new system, our ability to travel could possibly be limited almost overnight."

"You could be right, Mike, but I still don't see that we have any other choice. I think we have to continue with what Paige has set up and hope for the best as we go." Alter had a point and the other two knew it. The drive to Miami had been long and they were tired, so they decided to turn in.

To save money, they had gotten only one hotel room and had just asked for a cot to be brought in. Mike took the cot.

The messenger going into Prime Minister Corsetti's office was a bit relieved with the news he was bringing. The news was about the temple construction in Israel. The work was ahead of schedule and the temple should be operational within the year.

Marco was incredibly pleased with the news and politely dismissed the messenger who left with a sigh of relief. Marco rose from his desk and walked over to look at the world map on the wall. It was a large map that almost took up the entire wall. All of the countries were shaded in different colors to show the borders. One by one he had placed a silver star on each country as it joined the order. Soon maps like this would only be used in history lessons to show children what the world used to look like in the time of division. Very soon a world map would consist of only one color. He liked the color silver. Maybe that would be the color he would tell the companies who made the map to produce them in the future.

The news that the messenger brought about the progress on the Jewish temple was very encouraging to him, although his reasons for wanting to make Israel an ally had changed. Originally Israel was a means to get to the U.S., but the nuclear war caused him to change his tactics. That change of tactics not only brought the U.S. into the order, but almost the rest of the world along with them.

Israel, on the other hand, had become very appealing with its advancements in energy and newly found oil reserves. His scientists had also one remarkably interesting bit of information. Israel was the only known country whose women were still giving birth. More specifically, it was the Jewish women who were still able to get pregnant and give birth. That, in and of itself, was a puzzle worth finding out more about. Why, out of all the people on the earth, were the Jews seemingly unaffected by the plague? Another question that naturally came from that was, had the Jews done something to cause the plague and would they, in time, by attrition, become the only people left on the earth? Although it was an unthinkably horrible thing to consider, it was also the type of strategy he could appreciate.

Yes, they were the next chess piece to take off the board.

After spending the night in a Miami hotel, the soon to be fugitives got up early the next morning to go meet with the ship's captain and then get settled on board the ship.

Edward Gilmore was the ship's captain. He was a thin man who looked to be in his late fifties. He was bald with a neatly trimmed salt and pepper beard. They met him on the bridge of the cargo ship. For Mike and Alter, this was the first time they had ever been on board a ship like this. Although Mike had been on a cruise ship before when he and Julie had taken a cruise to the Bahamas years ago, this ship was vastly different from the one he had been on, at least what he could remember seeing. The bridge was located atop the ship, and inside, it was surrounded by floor to ceiling windows, giving a breathtaking panoramic view. A type of desk stretched almost across the width of the bridge with three separate chairs bolted to the floor indicating different workstations. Each station had multiple flat computer screens and a dizzying array of controls.

Captain Gilmore smiled at them when they walked in and spoke to Paige. "I almost expected to hear from you that the visit had to be rescheduled because of the peace news."

Paige smiled and said, "Not at all. As a matter of fact, the effects of the war on different industries like yours will go right in line with the reasons for the drastic steps that have been taken to bring us to peace. All of these stories are interwoven, and I believe they will all work in concert to create a very intriguing narrative."

The captain nodded his head in agreement and then switched his attention to Mike and Alter. "You told me that there would be three of you coming, and I'm okay with that. It's just that I don't understand why. Are these two supposed to be your bodyguards?"

Paige looked to Alter and motioned for him to answer the captain's question. The three of them had gone over their cover story so many times the last two days that any of them could rattle it off in their sleep. "We are going to be co-writing the story with Paige. Each of us will individually write our own story from different perspectives, then we will fuse the stories into one. Each one of us has strengths that will complement the group effort."

Anyone who understood how journalism worked would laugh at that explanation, but they were counting on the captain to be completely oblivious, and he was, so it worked.

The captain smiled and said, "Well let's go get your things, and I'll show you where your new home will be for the next few weeks." Then the captain explained to them that even though the ship had been originally built to host a crew of twenty, modern innovations made it so that the ship now operated very efficiently with a crew of just eight. Each of them was given a private room. Each room had a twin-sized bed with a desk built into the adjoining wall and a desk chair bolted into the steel floor. Once they got their gear stowed in their rooms, the captain took them on a quick tour of the ship, showing them the galley and then a room that had been converted into a place where crew members could get together. They called it the rec-room, but it was more of a quiet lounge. Paige was a little relieved to find out that two of the crew members were female. Knowing she was not going to be alone with ten men out in the middle of nowhere made her feel a little better. Even though she trusted Alter and Mike with her life, there was just an unexplainable feeling of comfort in knowing that she would not be the only female on board.

"Now I feel I need to show you where the infirmary is. You may need to know where you can get some Dramamine if you find you need some. Once we are done with that, you will have a few hours before we cast off, so if there is any last-minute shopping you want to do, you might want to be quick about it."

After the brief tour, the captain excused himself, saying that he had to get back to the bridge, but if they had any needs or questions, all they had to do was ask. They thanked the captain and then went to their rooms. Each of them knew that this was going to be the easiest part of their journey. The ship was scheduled to dock in Morocco where the rest of their trip would become much more difficult. The plan was for them to slip off the ship once it docked and make the rest of their trip across Algeria, Libya, and Egypt. It would be a ten-hour flight from Morocco to Jordan and that would cost them almost everything they had left. Rather than the flight, they decided to take a chance that the borders would now be open, and that part of their journey could be overland.

The first week of the sea voyage was uneventful, and the three of them played their parts well. They interviewed crew members about the jobs that each of them had on a trip like this, and they talked to the captain about the changes in the different routes due to the nuclear war. In every way, they appeared to be a team of reporters working on a story. The sea was calm, and much to their relief, they found that none of them needed a dose of Dramamine.

They were all three in the galley having dinner when the captain approached their table. "I've got some good news," he said smiling pleasantly. "Because of the fair-weather we've had, we will be arriving in Morocco in three days, which will be earlier than scheduled. Once we get there, my company has arranged for us to take advantage of one of the transition stations there in Morocco. When I let them know that you were with us, I was told that the people in the station will be able to electronically pull up your information and handle your transition as well. So once we get there, I'll have some documents to go over with the crew that will be waiting for us at the dock, and then we can all go as a group to the transition center." He patted Alter on the shoulder and walked on to his table.

Later that evening, the three of them came together in Mike's room. When they spoke, they kept their voices low enough that they would not be overheard by someone outside of the room.

"So how do we get away without drawing unwanted attention to ourselves?" Mike asked.

"I'm guessing it will have to do something with the magazine because the magazine was the reason we gave them for our being here in the first place," Paige put in.

"Well, we have about two days to come up with a plausible reason. I guess we will have to make it look like we are contacting someone at the office and for some reason, they ask us to go to another spot while we are in Morocco," Alter said.

"Yeah, like that sounds really believable," Paige said sarcastically.

"It doesn't have to be all that believable. It just has to cause enough of a confused reaction for us to get away."

In the end, they agreed on a plan that might not work all that great but might cause enough doubts so they could leave with their luggage once in Morocco. They also knew that the cash they had with them would quickly become useless as this new system tightened its grip around the throat of the world. It was unnerving to see how fast everything was developing.

When they pulled into port, Paige put the plan into action by telling the captain that she needed to get to a phone to get in contact with her office. She then came back and, in the captain's presence, told Alter and Mike that the office wanted them to stay in Morocco a few more days to work on a different angle of the story before coming back. At first, the two men grumbled and complained about the extended stay until Paige told them that the office was going to put them on a commercial flight back home so they would be back quicker than expected. At that statement, Mike and Alter eagerly agreed and started to leave to get their things out of the room.

The plan surprisingly worked easily enough for them until the captain said, "Sounds like that's settled. I guess we will say our goodbyes once we all finish up at the transition center."

It was Mike who spoke next sounding surprisingly natural. "Great, we'll go get our stuff packed. Give me the location of the center. That way we don't get lost finding it."

The captain who had no suspicions told them it was in Casablanca, and that he would write down the street address for them.

Paige, who was very relieved at how quickly Mike had responded, added, "Casablanca? I've only heard of it through movies, and now I get to actually see it."

"I've been there many times. I always spend some time there when we have a layover. I would be happy to take you on a tour once we are done at the transition center. All three of you." The captain added that last bit not wanting to sound like he just meant Paige. Then he walked to the desk, got a piece of paper, wrote down the address, and handed it to Paige. "I'll see you there," he said.

The three of them went back to their rooms, packed their backpacks, and left. Once off the ship, they started looking for a way that they could board passage to Israel.

Although things were falling into place around the world, there were still those pockets of resistance that cropped up in different areas. In some parts of the world, groups were getting together to stage protests claiming that the New World Order was nothing more than a dictatorship bent on world domination.

Mechanisms were already in place that was designed to deal with the inevitability that groups like this would come into existence. A strike was executed on one of the meeting areas of a protest group in Egypt. It was however very different in its execution. None of the strike team wore any kind of uniform. Some of them carried signs with slogans like 'New World Dis-Order' and 'Bring an end to Tyranny'. Other members of the strike team were posing as civilians carrying no weapons. They just had cell phones and filmed everything with their phones. Then the strike team with the signs started throwing what looked like homemade Molotov cocktails into the building where the real protesters were meeting. There was nothing homemade about these 'Cocktails'. They were a device called a vacuum bomb, a type of explosive that uses oxygen from the surrounding air to generate a high-temperature explosion, and in practice, the blast wave typically produced by such a weapon is of a significantly longer duration than that produced by a conventional condensed explosive.

Everyone in the building died within seconds of the bombs going off. The 'homemade' videos were fed to the news agencies who were themselves a willing part of the new government. In one stroke a group of protesters were killed and then blamed for their own deaths. Now, thanks to the news feed from the cell phones, those who spoke out against the 'Order' were looked at by the general population as either supporting terrorists or being terrorists themselves. Even in the ranks of the government, the details of the event with the protesters went completely unknown by most of the government employees.

CHAPTER EIGHTEEN

W HEN Egypt accepted the invitation to join the New World Order, the Mukhabarat, the Egyptian secret service, was absorbed into the world system, and now Sabacon was a high-ranking interrogator in the new order. His efforts were helping to find and eliminate rebel bases.

He was a little surprised when he was assigned to work with an engineer who was working on something called microbots. The name alone sounded like something out of a Sci-fi novel. He hoped they could come up with a better name for whatever this guy was working on. When he heard about his new workgroup, Sabacon thought someone had made a personnel mistake and he was supposed to be with another group. He found out soon enough that they wanted him to make some changes in the serum he had developed. The idea was to have a delivery system for the serum with the microbots. What they wanted was to condense the serum to have several doses per bot. The bots looked like a miniature version of an aerial drone. It was as small as a hummingbird and had three propellers. A device that could be used to shoot was on the rear of the drone, making the whole thing look like a flying scorpion. With the help of Sabacon and his serum, it would have a sting infinitely worse than that of a scorpion.

His orders were to make a serum that would cause intense pain but not kill. The plan was to be able to capture these people. Once captured, they would be given a choice of either joining and becoming slave labor or facing execution. Sabacon wondered out loud why they could not just render the people unconscious and then implant the microchip in them while they were out. It was explained to him that these people would then be destroyed mentally by forcing them to choose the transition themselves and would then be easier to control.

The task was then to condense the serum to a point that a scorpion could shoot multiple injections. His first thought was to work on finding out how much sedative he could take out of the mix and still maintain a non-lethal injection. There was also the weight of the subject to take into consideration. If they were too heavy, then it wouldn't be totally incapacitating, and if they were too light, the injection could possibly kill them. Then there was the problem of condensing the serum and maintaining its properties.

After several weeks and hundreds of tests, he finally had a serum that would work consistently on anyone between a hundred fifty pounds and two-fifty, and each microbot could carry a payload of five shots.

The name scorpion had caught on with the rest of the team, so that's what they were called. Another reason they wanted non-lethal injections was that they wanted the ability to interrogate these people and find out where the others were hiding. To do that they wanted to be able to subdue them without risking any of their own men. Also, the psychological after-effects the serum had would make interrogation more effective.

The scorpions were going to be used against rebel hideouts to neutralize this insanity. The engineers had also developed something called swarm technology that sounded like it was going to be incredibly useful against these terrorists.

The swarm technology of the scorpions was quite an accomplishment. If a scorpion came across a hideout, it would send out a microwave signal that could be read by other scorpions up to five miles away. The other scorpions would fly in armed and be able to engage the rebels without the need for a controller to tell it where to go or what to do. They would be able to act in unison like a swarm of bees.

Sabacon was proud of the part he played in this work. The government called these people rebels, but as far as he was concerned, they were terrorists. He felt good about the role he would play in bringing these animals to justice. The world was finally headed to lasting peace and these people were bent on destroying all the progress that had been made.

CHAPTER NINETEEN

T HE three of them had planned on having to spend some of their time traveling on foot, so rather than suitcases, they used backpacks. They divided the cash and each of them carried a portion in their pack, along with any items they agreed would be essential or helpful. The packs were a bit heavy because they had converted their paper cash into gold coins thinking the coins would be more easily accepted. They didn't dare try to bring any kind of weapon because of the scrutiny they knew they would have to go through. They trusted God would see them through this.

Once they left the cargo ship, Alter had an idea and told Mike and Paige. "You know we could look for an Israeli fishing boat and ask to join them. Even though Israel is an ally of The New World Order right now, they haven't become part of the Order, so we could use our coins or even convert them over to Israeli shekels."

"If we could do that it would make things simpler," Mike said.

"How do we know if a fishing boat is Israeli?" Paige asked.

"We'll have to talk to the different crews and just ask around."

With that, they headed off towards the docks where most of the fishing boats were, which was less than a mile from the port they were in now.

The difference between the fishing port and where the cargo ships were docked was like entering into a completely different world. It was a complete mass of confusing activity. The boats ranged in size from small fishing boats with a crew of no more than three to larger boats that looked like they had a crew of around twenty men. Many of them were speaking in their own language to each other. The few English words that were heard were all spoken with a heavy, unintelligible accent. After only a few minutes,

Mike was thinking that this was hopeless until Alter got their attention. "I think that's where we need to start," he said, pointing to a large fishing ship. "The writing on that ship is Hebrew. It says Toqeph, which means strength."

Thanks to Alter's ability to speak both Hebrew and Aramaic, they were able to talk to the captain. Alter explained to the captain that the three of them had taken some time away from their jobs to go on an adventure and see the world from a perspective that no tourist saw the world. He also told the captain that he had promised his two friends that they would be able to see Israel, the land of his birth. He promised that they would be willing to work to earn passage. In the end, the captain agreed to have them aboard but warned them they would have to work to earn their keep. He also told them that there were two more stops before reaching Israel and if they did not do their share of the work, with no hesitation, he would leave them at one of the ports. He let them know that there would be no special allowances for the girl. The ship was not set up to handle females on the crew, so she would have to bunk with the rest of the men. Paige was fine with that arrangement, knowing that the chances of any kind of unwanted advancement would be lower around a crowd than if she were in any kind of isolated area.

They were informed that the ship would be headed out to sea early the next morning. They were given a list of things they would need to have to do the work they would be assigned such as rubber boots and work gloves. Luckily there was a supply store very near the port where they could get everything they needed. Afterwards, they could go ahead and join the deckhands where they would be put to work. Since a couple of the deckhands spoke a little English, it made communication easier for Mike and Paige.

Since this particular boat was a fishing trawler, it had a crew of twelve but could handle up to a crew of twenty, so the three of them were easily absorbed into the crew and given some menial jobs. They were given the tasks of attaching accessories, such as floats, weights, and markers to the nets and lines and pulling guide nets and lines onto the vessel, things that did not take a lot of training to be able to catch on. They learned very quickly that this was a very labor-intensive line of work. For the first two days at sea, as soon as their day was over, all they wanted to do was eat something and then go to sleep. They did get used to the work by the time the ship anchored at the first port. The ship was scheduled to be anchored there for three days. They were warned that the ship would cast off in exactly three days with or without the three of them. Since they had no reason to go sightseeing, the three of them finished their work for the day and stayed on the ship.

One of the crew members approached Alter, and for the sake of Mike and Paige, spoke in heavily accented English. "So why are you really trying to get to Israel?"

Mike and Paige didn't say anything, instead, they both waited quietly for Alter to respond. "Like I told your captain, Israel is the place of my birth, and I promised to show it to them."

"I think there is another reason. One that you don't tell anyone. Be careful." Then he said something in Hebrew and walked away. Alter watched him go with a strange expression on his face.

"What did he say as he walked away?" Paige asked.

Alter answered her while still watching in the direction the man went. "It's a blessing. He said, 'May the Lord bless you and keep you; the Lord make his face shine on you and be gracious to you; the Lord turn his face toward you and give you peace.' I think somehow he knows what we are doing."

"I know that blessing. Our pastor had a habit of speaking it over the congregation after the altar call as we were getting ready to leave. What do you think he meant by that?" Mike added.

"I want to think we have an ally, but I think we should be very careful. There may be others watching us who are not."

They didn't see that crew member again while the ship was in port. After the ship cast off, the captain sent for them. "I understand you didn't leave the ship while we were in port, so I assume you didn't hear any of the latest news?" he asked.

They all three shook their heads no and silently waited for him to say whatever it was he had planned to tell them. "It seems that there has been terrorist activity breaking out all over, and from the news reports, all of these groups are connected to each other. They have been killing a lot of innocent people all in the name of standing against The New World Order. Now we are an Israeli crew and even though Israel is not part of The New World Order, we are strong allies. As a matter of fact, Prime Minister Corsetti has sent over engineers scientists, and general labor to help my country rebuild Solomon's Temple, which is almost complete as we speak. Now these terrorists want to stop the progress that Prime Minister Corsetti is now making with The New World Order. One of the ways they are do-ing this is to refuse to participate in the transition process. I can't help but notice that none of you have gone through the transition process. May I ask why?"

This was the type of question they were prepared for. So, Paige spoke up with no hesitation. "We had already begun our travels before the transition centers were put in place, so we plan to find one as soon as we get back in the States."

The captain smiled with a look that was almost relief. "Well then you are in luck. Our last port before going back to Israel is in Alexandria. I will make sure the three of you will have plenty of time to find a transition center there before we leave port for Israel."

The three of them nodded and indicated that they agreed with the captain's plan. Something in his tone told them that what he said was a lot more than a suggestion.

The next two days at sea they did the work that was assigned to them and met with each other during meals and just before they went to sleep for the night. They didn't have much of a plan. They were just going to take their packs and leave the ship as soon as it reached port. Then if they had to, they would make the rest of their trip on foot.

As the ship pulled into Alexandria, the work they had as deckhands would not start until the next day. Each of them had their backpack and were out on the deck as the ship was being docked. Then out of the corner of his eye Alter saw the deckhand who had approached them a few days ago and decided to go speak with him. He told Mike and Paige that he was going to talk to the man and that he would be right back, and they could leave.

The deckhand smiled as Alter walked towards him. "Our next port brings you to your destination," he said to Alter.

"Yes, it does, and if you don't mind, I have a few questions I would like to ask you."

The man casually glanced around and then answered Alter's questions before he could ask them. "Three Americans trekking across the globe incognito? Anyone in their right mind will know that there's a lot more to your story than what you are telling. That's why I told you to be careful. I spoke the blessing over you because none of you have the mark."

The matter-o-fact way the man said that took Alter completely by surprise and left him speechless. Seeing the shocked look on Alter's face made the man laughed quietly. "It's okay. Come with me. I have something to show you."

Alter turned and waved at Mike and Paige and then held his hand palm up to let them know he wanted them to wait there. He followed the mysterious deckhand back towards the crew quarters.

CHAPTER TWENTY

Prime Minister Marco Corsetti spent the morning listening to briefings by his staff on the progress that had been made by each division of the Order. He was not concerned with the small details. He was more concerned with how they all worked together to move towards the ultimate goal. That goal was to have the people of the world be united as one people, ultimately bringing on an everlasting global peace.

Later that afternoon, he had some time scheduled to meet with his friend Lorenzo Russo who had officially been made head of his personal security. Unofficially, Lorenzo was in charge of a great deal more than personal security. He went back over the report that had been brought to him on the progress of the temple being built in Jerusalem. It was near completion, and by all accounts, the work was moving along uninterrupted.

Why were these Jews so insistent on worshiping some ancient idea of a god? He thought it impossible for them to believe that there was any kind of all-powerful being other than mankind. It was obvious that their leaders knew this and used the misguided beliefs of the people to control them. Throughout history, all of the ancient religions from before the time of the Babylonians up to the modern age had invented gods and used the belief in those gods to rule the people.

People were finally starting to see and accept the truth that man was the only god in this world. The only people who dogmatically held on to a belief that there was a supreme being other than mankind were the Jews. Even the Christians, who would give lip service to a god, would not act against their common sense in some act of blind faith. With the influence of Lorenzo Russo, the Muslims decided not to rebuild their temple after its destruction and began to walk away from their faith.

Then, sitting there looking at the report, the thought struck him that this Jewish faith could and would crumble if the object of their faith was destroyed.

With Muslims, the destruction of the Dome of The Rock and the subsequent failure to rebuild it set them on the path to rejecting their dogmatic beliefs. At the same time, though, the Jews' faith was being bolstered by this rebuilding of Solomon's Temple. Stopping construction or razing it down to the ground would not work because the temple itself had been wiped out by the ancient Roman empire. That only served to strengthen the resolve of the Jewish people. There had to be something that could be done to erode their belief in this god of theirs. He made a mental note to discover more about this religion of theirs. He knew that something in the religion itself would give him the information he needed to destroy it.

The phone on his desk buzzed. He reached over and pushed the intercom button. "Yes, Angie?"

"Praefect Russo is here for your meeting."

"Thank you, Angie, have him come in."

Lorenzo Russo walked in, smiling warmly at his friend. Marco got up, walked around the desk, and hugged Lorenzo. The two of them sat down in two plush chairs with a round table between them facing the fireplace. "It's almost scary my friend how well and smoothly things are working for you."

"Lorenzo, what on earth do you mean? We have not made one move without first meticulously planning every possible angle. Even the fanatics who oppose us are far fewer than we anticipated, and thanks to the theatrics you have orchestrated, the general public is afraid of them."

"Speaking of these fanatics, I suggest that we initiate public executions."

Marco thought about the suggestion his friend just made. It could accomplish two distinct goals. The first would be to establish fear in the hearts of the fanatics, causing them to give up on their plans and then join the Order. The second would be to sway the fears of the public and create a feeling of security for them, making them mentally indebted to the Order.

"That is a good suggestion, my friend. It will not take me long to put that into motion. What's troubling me even more than those few fanatics is the question of how to defeat the Jewish faith. I'm afraid that with their faith intact, they will never wholly join with us."

Lorenzo paused slightly and then said, "Whatever you decide, I would suggest that it be something very public."

"I agree, and I've been thinking about that. I think that not only should it be public, but it should also be something that will discredit their faith." He got up and walked to a phone on his desk and gave his secretary a number to dial and told her the patch the call through as soon as she could get it done.

Lorenzo had a confused look on his face and Marco explained, "We are almost finished with the building of the Jewish temple. I want an exact day and time for when it will be complete. You see, in Jewish mythology, only a priest who has been ceremonially cleansed can enter the place in the temple they call the Holy of Holies. If not, then their god will strike that person dead right then and there. When the temple is complete, I will enter this Holy of Holies and proclaim that there is no god other than mankind. When I do not die, then the faith of most will be shattered and that will begin the movement towards the unity we all seek. There will be some who will doggedly hold on to their pitiful faith, but they will be easily dealt with."

Lorenzo Russo smiled at the thought of over a million Jews losing their faith in an antiquated religion. That would help things to continue to move along smoothly. He was still amazed at how quickly and smoothly his friend had acquired so much power. "So should I move forward with the public executions?"

"Absolutely, and you may tell anyone who questions you on the matter that you have my blessing on your decision. Feel free to bring in as many people as you see fit on your plan and then give them the power to make the decisions that need to be made. I don't want our progress to be held up by a chain of command. I am confident that with the power of the beast in our control and the people's realization of the extent of that power, my objectives will be reached enthusiastically."

Just then the phone on Marco's desk buzzed. They were about to get that date of the finishing of the temple.

CHAPTER TWENTY-ONE

A LTER had just stepped out of sight when Mike and Paige heard a man's voice behind them. "Where is your friend?"

It was the captain with another man they had never seen standing next to him. This man was very obviously not part of the crew. He was wearing what looked like a perfectly tailored black suit, and he had a military-style haircut.

Mike and Paige were instantly uncomfortable by his presence and both of them felt like they should flee, but neither one of them did. Mike, despite the alarms going off in his head, spoke first, with a questioning look on his face. "We haven't seen him. Is something wrong?"

The captain, ignoring Mike's question, looked down at the three backpacks leaning against the railing. "By the looks of those packs, I would say he was just here. If you were just going to the transition center and then returning to the ship, why do you have your packs with you?"

Just then the guy in the suit motioned to three other men and they all stepped forward. Looking at Mike and Paige he spoke, "I'm going to need you to get your bags and come with us. Captain, may we use the ship's bridge?" He spoke with an American accent that had a hint of a southern drawl, which seemed very much out of place in Alexandria.

Seeing they were hemmed in by the men the guy with the suit had motioned, Mike and Paige picked up their backpacks. The man in the suit motioned to Mike. "You'll need to carry that one as well," he said, pointing to the third backpack. Mike put his pack on and then picked up Alter's pack, and the group of them headed towards the bridge, while deckhands watched them with confused looks.

When they got to the bridge, one of the men set up a laptop and attached a handheld scanner to it.

"Since you haven't transitioned, I'm going to need to see some form of ID."

Mike and Paige felt like they were in some kind of surreal movie and neither one of them responded.

"It's your choice, you can either give me some ID, like a driver's license or something, or I can have my men search your person until we find them."

Mike and Paige nervously got out their driver's licenses and handed them to him. He took the licenses and scanned each one of them. It produced a split-screen on the laptop. He took what felt like hours going over the information on the screen. It actually took a very long few minutes while everyone stood quietly waiting for him to say something. When he did speak, he didn't look up from the computer screen. "The two of you are a long way from home, aren't you? There's a missing person's report on file for the two of you." He paused. "And for a Mr. Alter Cagan. I'm guessing he's the third member of your little party."

Mike and Paige glanced at each other, neither saying anything.

Alter had been following the deckhand back towards the crew quarters when there was a commotion behind them. He turned around to see Mike and Paige being surrounded by some men he knew were not part of the ship. Instinctively, he started to head toward them, when an iron grip on his arm turned him around. It was the deckhand he had been with. "If you go that way, you won't be able to help them. You will only be taken yourself. The only chance you have of helping them is to come with me."

A wave of panic and confusion rose up in him. He had to go to his friends, but he knew by the crowd of men surrounding them that he would be grossly outnumbered, and they were likely armed. He was sure they were, and he not only didn't have a gun but even if he did, he didn't know how to use one. In that confused state of mind, he found himself accepting what this strange deckhand told him.

"You must come this way with me," he said as he turned to the spot where the fish were being unloaded. Alter followed him and they left the ship that way.

Once they were off the ship and among the crowd on the docks, he looked back at the ship in time to see Mike and Paige being escorted off the ship. Alter's feeling of panic turned into a wave of despair and guilt. He took a step back towards the ship and the deckhand grabbed his arm and stopped him. Alter's despair turned into anger at this man who had just led him off the ship. "We can't just leave them, they're my friends."

The man did not let go of his arm. "If the two of us rushed up there now, we would either be killed or captured. I know where they are taking your friends. We can get some help and attempt a rescue." That sliver of hope gave Alter the ability to keep following the man.

As soon as they were away from the docks and further into the city of Alexandria, the man led him to an outdoor cafe and had him take a seat at one of the tables. "You must always appear casual in public. People do not notice you that way."

The deckhand motioned for the waitress and then ordered some coffee for both of them. "My name is Hiskiel, and like you, I have never been on a fishing trawler before this. I think we may have some other things in common as well."

The waitress brought them the coffee and asked if they wanted anything else. Neither of them did, so she moved on to the next table.

Alter didn't know what to do next. The world he had once known had been spinning wildly out of control over the last year. Then today it had completely fallen apart, and here he was sitting at an outdoor cafe in Alexandria having coffee with a stranger who up until now he thought was a deckhand on an Israeli fishing trawler. He said the first thing that came to mind. "Why were you on the trawler?"

The man smiled at him and then said, "That is a long story, that I will be happy to tell you, but first I need to ask you a simple question. Who is Messiah?"

That was the question Alter truly did not expect. He didn't answer, he just stared at the man with his mouth open. Hiskiel waited for a few seconds before speaking again. "I can see the discomfort you are in, so let me ask from a different angle. We Jews have been waiting for the coming of Messiah, but for two thousand years, there have been those who say that Messiah has already come. For most of my life, I have believed that those people were misguided. What do you believe?"

In one way, Alter was very uncomfortable with the questions. At the same time, something inside him was telling him to trust this man. He looked down at the coffee he had not touched and then back at Hiskiel. "Yeshua is Messiah."

Hiskiel smiled and leaned forward slightly. "Now I will tell you how I came to join the crew of the Toqeph. Up until the time of the quickening I was a Rabbi in Israel."

"You don't look like a Rabbi. I know it's not required, but I've never known a Rabbi who didn't wear a kippah, and I've never known of one who would work in manual labor."

"I am no longer a Rabbi. You see, I had a couple of close Christian friends. Because these people were also Jewish, they were looked at by most of my contemporaries as traitors. I was advised to cut all ties with these people, but I couldn't bring myself to do that." He paused and sipped his coffee. "Unfortunately for me, our ties were broken on the day of the quickening. I believe you Americans refer to the event as the rapture of the church. No matter what you call it, on that day, life on this earth changed. It didn't take much research for me to discover the one thing that all of these people had in common."

"They were Christian." Alter said.

"Yes." He nodded his head and then continued. "I shared my thoughts with some others and the idea was laughed at. They truly thought I was trying to have a joke at their expense. I felt like I was living a lie, so I left the priesthood and started looking for something else."

"So that's how you came to work as a crew member of a fishing ship? That is a pretty big leap." Alter said with a tone of incredulity.

"No, actually, because I am multilingual, I became a tour guide. Over the last year, I have met several people who see the truth as I do. As a tour guide, I began to meet more people in different industries who could also see the truth. My connections grew very slowly, which made sense because the quickening had taken away everyone who was a true follower of the Messiah. The only people left were the few, who like myself, had followed the wrong path, or the rest of the world who blissfully lived in deception."

"So how did you end up on a fishing boat in Morocco?" Alter asked, wanting to know how and why a former Jewish Rabbi ended up as a deckhand on a fishing boat that he, Mike, and Paige just happened to choose as their way to Jordan.

"I was led by the hand of God, just like you and your friends were led. Nothing happens by accident. A fellow believer is one of the officers on the Toqeph, and one night when we were praying, I felt a strong compulsion to ask him if there was a way for me to join the crew on their next excursion. He said he could get me on as a deckhand, but this next trip was going to be the longest one they had ever gone on. If I wanted to join the crew, it may be better for me to wait until the following trip. The compulsion I felt was very strong, so I told him that this is the trip I had to make. He will be joining us soon and then we will work out a plan to rescue your friends."

Hiskiel went on to tell Alter about the group of believers he had aligned himself with and how they were preparing for the time when Prime Minister Corsetti would turn against the Israelis. Being a former Rabbi, he was familiar with the type of studying he needed to do to be aware of what was happening and what to expect.

Alter explained that he also had a very good friend who had learned the truth and became a Christian. He let Hiskiel know that his friend had passed on a lot of study material to prove that Yeshua was truly Messiah. After the rapture, Alter couldn't help but to go back through the information he had been given. It didn't take long for him to accept the truth of what had happened. Now through a series of twists and turns, he found himself sitting at one of the tables of an outdoor cafe in Alexandria, Egypt, not knowing how to save his friends.

They were only there a few minutes before another man Alter recognized from the fishing ship walked up and joined them. Hiskiel smiled and got up to shake hands with the man. Then he looked at Alter and said, "This is my friend, Joseph, who I told you about." Then he looked at Joseph and asked, "Do you have the location of where they were taken?"

"Yes, they are at a detention center not too far from here. We should have a few days. I also have a place where we can talk freely."

They took Mike and Paige to a large concrete building that looked like it was a war bunker. It was gray and had only one visible door and very few windows. Once inside, they were taken to a windowless room that had a metal table with some chairs around it in the center. The men forced them to sit at the table. A man in uniform came in with a file folder in his hand and sat down across from them. "My friends, today is your lucky day," he said with a smile.

Mike and Paige glanced at each other without saying anything, and then looked back at the man in uniform.

"I am General Husani. Let me assure you that you will soon be back at home resting peacefully. You did not know this, but your traveling companion, Alter Cagan, is a known criminal and you are very fortunate that we interceded when we did." He paused. "There have been others that were not so fortunate."

Mike didn't know how to react. He had expected to be tortured, but this truly caught him off guard. Did these people really believe that Alter was some sort of criminal? Of course, Mike knew that Alter was a criminal, but so were he and Paige. These people were trying the divide and conquer routine.

"We need to find Mr. Cagan and bring him in for questioning. You can help us by getting in touch with him."

Paige spoke up next. "So you want us to set up some kind of meeting so you can get him there?"

General Husani looked at her with a patronizing smile "Nothing like that. Just call him and let him know that you are here at the office of the World Order in Egypt, that's all."

"Then we just go home?" she asked.

"We have a car that will take you to the airport. You will be home by tomorrow morning."

Paige looked at Mike. "At least we know Alter got away. General, I can tell you now that you are wasting your time."

"She's right General. There's no way we're going to help you." Mike added.

General Husani stood up slowly and looked at them. "I'm sorry to see you respond in this way. In order to change your response, I'm afraid we will have to change our approach. Just so you know, it really didn't have to go this way."

With that, he spoke to the guards in what Mike could only guess was Egyptian, then walked out of the room. The four remaining guards took Mike and Paige, separated them, and took them in opposite directions. Mike was placed into what he could only assume was a holding cell for prisoners. It was a small windowless room with no furniture. There were some chains attached to the wall on the opposite side of the door. The guards pushed him toward that back wall and in broken English, they told him to strip down and kick his clothes towards the door. He stripped down to his underwear and kicked the clothes toward the door. The guards laughed and then said, "All the clothes."

He took off his underwear and cringed at the thought that Paige was going through this as well. Once that was done, one of the guards came over and put the shackles that were hanging on the wall behind him on his ankles and wrists. Then they left him alone there in the cell.

He didn't know how long he was alone in the cell. His nerves were frazzled as he started pacing back and forth in the short distance the chains allowed him to. He was frantic worrying about what Paige could be going through. She had become like a second daughter to him. He couldn't help but feel responsible for her.

After what felt like days but was probably more like several hours, the blaring music they had been playing suddenly stopped and the door opened. A man wearing a lab coat walked in. Behind him came two others carrying a table with several things on it. On the table were a pair of pliers, a syringe with a vial of something next to it, a scimitar, and a car battery with some jumper cables. Mike knew the torture was about to start.

CHAPTER TWENTY-TWO

THE place Joseph was talking about was a low-cost hotel. Even though Egypt was an official member of the New World Order, because of their proximity to Israel and the allegiance between Israel and the New World Order, Israeli shekels were still accepted. All of Alter's cash was in the backpack that had been taken by the officers who took Mike and Paige, so he had to swallow some pride and accept the help offered by Hiskiel and Joseph.

"I need to let you know that this is going to be very difficult at best and it could be downright suicidal," Joseph said as he put some photos on the table. They were sitting in the hotel room Joseph had gotten. They had taken the nightstand and moved it between the beds to use as a table.

The pictures were of the detention center that Mike and Paige had been taken to. The center was a squat building located by itself in the desert landscape just outside of the city. "The rest of the team will be here soon. Hopefully between all of us we will be able to come up with a working plan."

The location of the building was a problem in that there were no other structures close to it that anyone could hide in, so the approach to the building would have to be out in the open in plain sight. Another problem was that Egypt was part of the New World Order so anyone delivering supplies had been transitioned and had the mark. The entry gate would not open to someone without the mark.

The mark was not something that could be faked. It was already almost invisible to the eye, but it interacted with the central network of the Order. This network was so big and all-encompassing that everyone had accepted the nickname "The Beast" that had been given to it by Prime Minister Corsetti.

Once the team Joseph had mentioned got together, several ideas were put forth. The first idea someone mentioned was to cut the power and then storm in during the confusion. The problem was that power was being supplied through an underground cable that originated somewhere in the power plant that supplied power to all of Alexandria. Even if they could find the right power cables, the center undoubtedly had backup generators that were designed to come online immediately in the event of a power outage.

One thing that gave Alter a slight amount of hope was that this team Joseph had mentioned weren't simply Israelis that had seen the truth, but they were a group of highly trained commandos known as the Sayeret Matkal. They made up a unit called the Flying Snakes, and they specialized in all types of combat. Knowing they had very little time to devise a plan and execute it, they gravitated quickly to a daring plan that unfortunately would place Alter in a vulnerable position. He agreed to his part without hesitation. He was willing to do anything it took to be a part of the rescue of Mike and Paige.

The plan started that night as soon as it got dark. At night, even with the security lights of the center bathing light in multiple directions, the desert landscape provided small pockets of cover. Moving with incredible patience, four commandos crept towards the building. They moved very slowly from one small impression in the ground to another. These impressions were so slight, it was likely they would have never been seen in the bright Egyptian daylight even by the trained eye. Security lights on the center helped the commandos find them from the slight shadows each depression cast because of the angle of the light. They had to go painfully slow because even slight movements would be seen by the watchmen at the detention center. The training these commandos had in stalking adversaries would easily rival that of the ancient American Indian and it was paying off tonight. Their ability to slowly creep up on a target undetected in an area where there was seemingly no cover was unbelievable. Each of them had netting that they could cover himself with once he was in place so that from the naked eye, they would look like no more than a mound of sand. The plan was for each man to locate himself in a natural indention. If that could be done, each of them would blend in with the ground almost perfectly.

Most camouflage works best when you give the target another direction to look, and that was going to be the job of Alter and Hiskiel. They were the best choice for this particular job, because being a distraction did not require military training. The four commandos hiding themselves on the ground and a fifth commando perched on a small hill two hundred yards off with a sniper rifle were going to do most of the work as well as provide cover for the two distractions. Hiskiel was dressed in a Israeli military uniform and Alter was dressed as himself.

An hour after sunrise, the two of them rode in a jeep toward the detention center. Through a loudspeaker, the guard ordered them to stop which they did. Hiskiel got out of the driver's seat, opened the back door, pulled Alter out, then turned towards the gate and yelled. "I believe you are looking for this man."

The plan was for them to get the attention of the guard at the gate and have him come out to where Hiskiel was holding Alter. Many things could go wrong. One thing that could go wrong was that the guard could come out with a force way too large for the four commandos hidden under the sand to overpower.

In fictional stories, things like this always worked themselves out for the heroes. Something always happened at the last minute to help the heroes save the day. The problem was this was not a fictional story. In real life, units like the Flying Snakes had learned that if you wanted to survive you had to be able to act and react on the fly, because human beings were always unpredictable.

The guard's voice came back over the loudspeaker. "Drop your weapon and state the name of the unit you are attached to."

"I cannot drop my weapon while I'm holding this prisoner. I'm with the flying snakes."

There was no immediate response. Then after a few seconds, the gate opened, and two people came out with guns trained on Hiskiel and Alter. "Drop your weapon or die," one of them said.

Hiskiel dropped his rifle. The two men approached with their weapons aimed at Hiskiel and Alter. As soon as they walked past the spot where the first two commandos were hidden, the commandos came up off the ground moving much faster than most people would believe a human can move. Each of them took hold of a guard and brought him down. Then one of the things that could go wrong, went wrong.

The people inside the detention center, instead of sending just two men out armed with rifles ordered a third man to stay behind in the guard tower with a sniper rifle. The commando sitting in a nest some two hundred and fifty yards away did not see the man until it was a fraction too late. Two shots rang out simultaneously, one from the guard in the tower and one from the commando in the sniper nest.

By the truck, the other two commandos who were a little beyond the spot where the first two jumped up to take down the guards, were up and moving quickly to join them when the shots rang out. They changed course, and one of them jumped on Alter and pulled him down to the ground. Someone yelled, "Sniper down." Instantly, Alter felt himself being pulled up roughly and shoved into the back of the truck.

The jeep was what the military calls a six-pack because of the number of people it was designed to carry, but now it was very cramped because there were seven men, most of them with extra gear, squeezing into the truck, which included the four commandos along with Alter, Hiskiel, and one of the guards. The other guard was lying on the ground with his throat cut.

Hiskiel was lying across Alter's lap taking very short breaths. The commando sitting next to Alter tore open the jacket Hiskiel had on revealing an ugly wound in his side. One of the two shots they heard had hit Hiskiel. The jeep took off with more shots coming from the guard tower. Hiskiel died in the jeep looking up at Alter.

Alter was in a state of complete shock. He had never seen someone die before, and to make it worse, Hiskiel died in his arms while they were trying to save him. Scenes like this were what his parents had tried to avoid when they had moved to America when he was a child. Now, something told him that this sense of fear and dread would probably be with him from now until the day he suffered the same fate as Hiskiel.

He wasn't listening to what the men in the jeep were saying. He knew that they were on the move to somewhere. He didn't know or care where that was.

When the jeep did stop, he realized that they were back at the motel they had started from. It was one of those cheaper motels where each room opened to the outside rather than an internal hallway. Two of the commandos carried the body of Hiskiel with his arms draping over their shoulders. It almost looked as if he were walking with them. Another two walked on either side of the guard they had taken with them. The door to the room opened and the fifth commando, the one who had been in the sniper's nest, came out of the room and held the door open while they all entered. They laid Hiskiel's body on the bed and put the bedspread over it. Then they turned their attention to the guard they had brought with them. They asked him several questions which Alter didn't hear, then suddenly one of them pulled out his knife and cut the guard's throat, and let the body fall to the floor.

"What did you do? We are followers of Messiah, not murderers!"

"I killed him because I don't want him to be able to give our enemy any information," he said, and then stepped closer to Alter and lowered his voice. "Men may change but God does not. He is the same God David followed when he cut the head off Goliath," the man said, glaring into Alter's face.

Joseph said, "I'm afraid it's no good trying again to rescue your friends. I'm sure they have a team out looking for us as we speak." He put his hand on Alter's shoulder. "I'm sorry but we have to go, now."

Alter couldn't believe what he had just heard. "No, we can't just give up. We have to regroup and try again."

"It's no good Alter. Because of what happened today, they will not only beef up security, but they will also start looking for us. We have to leave right away and make our way to Israel without delay."

"I can't leave without Mike and Paige."

Then without anyone saying a word, the team of Israeli commandos surrounded Alter. One of them knocked him unconscious, and then they loaded him into the sixpack and the entire group headed out.

CHAPTER TWENTY-THREE

THE man in the lab coat was Sabacon, and all the devices that were placed on the table were just for show to increase the subject's fear before the injection was administered.

"Well Mr. Reynolds, it seems that you and I have a few things we need to talk about today."

The two men put down the table, and one of them pointed his gun at Mike while the other grabbed Mike by the arm and straightened it out, while the man in the lab coat pulled a syringe out of the bag he was carrying. "I'm going to give you a small injection to get things started."

Mike tried to pull his arm away, but he couldn't move it. The man in the lab coat injected him with something and then said something in a foreign language to the man holding him by the arm. Immediately Mike felt a burning sensation going up his arm. It traveled all up his body, and when it felt like it got to his head, Mike's world became an intense burning pain. It was the worse pain he had ever felt in his life. Every inch of his body was on fire.

"Amazing isn't it?" the man with the lab coat said. "I developed this serum to be used in unmanned aerial drones against you rebels." He paused. "That should be something to see. This will last about an hour, so I'm going to visit Paige, and then I will come back to see you and we'll talk." Then he walked out.

Sabacon was looking forward to his time with the American girl. All his life he had held a type of fascination for American girls because they were so different than women in the Middle East. The first notable difference was the way they looked. Middle Eastern women all had the same color hair, skin, and eyes. The only real differences were the way they dressed and talked. American women could be blond, brunette, or redheads and every shade between. Their eyes could be any color and so could the tone of their skin. But the real difference was in their personality. American women had this wild untamed nature about them that he wanted so much to break.

He had the two men with him to pick up the table to bring it with him and they left.

Paige was being kept at the other end of the building and it took them a few minutes to get there. Sabacon regretted the distance because he knew that the two rooms were out of earshot from each other. He wanted Mike Reynolds to hear the screams of his friend. He got to the cell door and opened it to see Paige sitting against the wall curled up. Even in this setting, she was beautiful to look at. She was toned, and he could tell that she wore a bikini because of the tan lines he could see on her naked body. The two others brought the table in with the tools on it, and he was pleased to see her reaction. It was obvious that she was very afraid of what was about to happen. If only she knew, she would be so much more than afraid. He turned to his two helpers. "You may leave," he said

"But sir, our orders are to." one of them started but Sabacon interrupted.

"I'm fine. After all, she's a woman, what could she possibly do? And you can be right outside the door. If I need anything, I'll call."

They left.

He looked over at her with a burning desire. "Get up and face me," he said.

She obeyed, and when she stood up his desire started to peak. "Walk over here."

She walked towards him until the chains stopped her. She stood looking at the floor.

"You see those tools on the table? They are for me to use in any way that I want in order to make you talk. That scimitar you see there at the end- it's razor-sharp. It would be very easy for me to use it to cut off your hand or foot. Or I could use the battery with the jumper cables. I could attach them to your breasts. The pinch from the clamps alone would be excruciating, but then the current from the battery would make you wish you were dead."

She started to cry, and that was the reaction he wanted. "But I don't have to use any of them. All you have to do is kiss me on the cheek and ask please don't."

She was still crying and said through the tears, "Please don't."

He smiled. "First you have to kiss me on the cheek and then ask me to please don't," Sabacon said, and then turned his cheek towards her. She leaned towards him and then he leaned his cheek closer. Then rather than feeling the light touch of her lips he expected, he felt a searing pain as she bit into his face. His reaction was instantaneous. He screamed and hit her solidly in the face with his fist, spilling her on the floor. His hand went to his face and it felt wet and warm from his blood. The door opened and the two guards rushed in as he grabbed the scimitar off the table. He could vaguely hear one of the guards yell something as he picked up the sword and looked at the girl on the floor. She had pulled herself up on her hands and knees. Blood was dripping out of her mouth and she was laughing. Rage flew over him, he was being laughed at... by a WOMAN! He swung the scimitar with all his strength. Within three blows, it was over.

Lab Coat Guy had been gone for a long time, so long that the pain had been gone for a while now. Mike had tested the length of the chains he was attached to and had drawn an imaginary line across the room that told him the limit of his range. Then after what felt like hours the door opened and there was Lab Coat Guy with his two henchmen. He was carrying something by his side, and his coat was covered in what looked like spattered blood. Mike backed up against the wall instinctively, and then he saw that the guy in the lab coat had walked across his imaginary line and tossed something at Mike's feet.

"Paige Summers says 'Hi,'" he sneered.

Mike looked down at the floor, and his world stopped turning. The thing that had been tossed at his feet was Paige's head. Her eyes looked unblinkingly at him.

Something inside of Mike snapped. It wasn't just Paige he saw. In his mind, it was Paige as well as Sarah and Julie. And the animal that had just tossed Paige's head at him was standing there sneering. A blind rage took over, and Mike sprang towards him.

Sabacon realized a split second too late that this man was not reacting to the serum in the same way all the test subjects in the past had reacted. Where the others had been terrified of him, this man was not.

The guard saw the prisoner move faster than humanly possible. He started to pull his gun up, but knew he wasn't in time.

Time seemed to slow down for Mike, he closed the gap between himself and his target instantly. With his left hand, he grabbed the guy's coat.

Then with his right hand, he formed the letter C with his fingers and his thumb. He struck the man right under the chin with all his strength, the thumb on one side of the man's Adam's apple, his fingers on the other. His hand went into soft flesh and then he squeezed and pulled.

Although the guard did not react fast enough to save Sabacon he was able to get off a burst of automatic fire at the man in the chains.

Mike suddenly saw a flash of white and then nothing.

Chapter Twenty-Four

"Hey, sleepyhead, are you going to stay in bed all day?" Mike knew he was dreaming, but the voice seemed so real that he thought that if he just opened his eyes, he would see Julie. He could feel a soft touch on his shoulder and the light tickle of her breath as if she were leaning in to kiss him. Then he felt the warm soft touch of lips on his cheek, and involuntarily his eyes opened instantly. He couldn't believe what he saw. Just a moment ago, he was in his cell, and that animal had thrown Paige's decapitated head at him. He remembered the flash of light he had seen. The guard must have shot him, and now he must be somewhere between life and death. Then he opened his eyes and saw Julie's face smiling down at him. This was the best feeling he had experienced in a long time. He knew she couldn't be real, and he almost watched in fear as she reached toward him. He thought she would evaporate just before her hand touched his face. But she didn't.

"What's wrong honey?"

He held her hand to his face and started to cry. Mike didn't know what had just happened. All he knew was that his wife was here with him and he had never been happier.

Julie's face showed concern. "Mike, you're kinda scaring me. Is there something wrong?"

"Nothing's wrong baby. Things couldn't be better. I'm the happiest I've ever been, and I've got so much I need to tell you."

"Okay," she paused briefly. "I just got off the phone with Sarah, and she's going to come over tonight for dinner. I was thinking, maybe we could make some pizza. How does that sound to ya?"

His mind was reeling. He was suddenly brought back to the last day he saw Julie and Sarah alive. He couldn't speak as he stared at his wife.

"Mike, there's obviously something on your mind what is it?"

"I'm sorry, it's just that I'm in a bit of a daze. I just need to pull myself together. Could you tell me what today's date is?"

She looked at him a little quizzically with concern still showing on her face. He knew what she was going to say but he still had to hear it for himself. Julie told him the date and it was the same date that the worldwide plague had hit. Mike's world was turning upside down on him and he had to figure out what was real and what was imagined. Something inside him told him that the last few years he had gone through were real, but somehow here he was, at the exact time that the world had begun a spiral into destruction. This could not be a coincidence, but right now looking at Julie, he no longer knew what was real. Then suddenly he knew what he needed to do.

"I've got a call that I need to make and then I will be able to make a little more sense of things, I think."

With that, he picked up his cell and dialed the number that he had memorized a long time ago, or at least he thought he had. The phone at the other end barely rang once before it was answered. "Mike?" asked the familiar voice on the other end of the line.

It was Paige. Based on the date, they should not even know each other yet, because in all reality they had never met.

"Paige, is your sister there with her daughter?"

"Yes, and so are your wife and daughter, right?"

"My wife Julie is here with me, and she said that she just talked to our daughter Sarah on the phone."

"What's happening?" she asked.

"I don't know, but I do think we all need to get together and talk this over. Could you come over here and bring your sister and niece with you? I'm going to call my daughter and ask her to come on over as quickly as she can."

"Yes, we will head out right away. I can hardly wait to meet them."

He hung up the phone and glanced at Julie, who had a look of curiosity on her face.

"Who was that on the phone?" she asked.

"That was a friend." He paused and couldn't help but chuckle a little, "who I technically haven't met yet." Then without waiting for a response he said, "Could you call Sarah back and ask her to come over now, rather than tonight?"

"She's got to go to work this morning," Julie answered.

"I know. Tell her that the news I've got is much more important than going to work. It's more important than anything else right now."

Julie gave him another very curious look and then picked up her phone to call Sarah. Mike thanked God for the warning he had received. He knew in his heart that he had been given one last chance, and he thanked God with every ounce of his being for that chance. Then, as if acting on impulse, he picked up his phone to make another couple of calls.

The first call was to the ambulance company to let them know that he wasn't going to come to work this evening. The next call was to Alter Cagan. He knew he had never called Alter before, but he also knew the number without even thinking about it, because he had actually called Alter countless times. It took three rings before Alter answered the phone.

"Mike?"

"Yes, it's me and because you knew it was me, we also know that we are not just waking up from a horrible dream"

There was a pause where neither of them said anything. Then Alter interrupted the silence. "This is the day it all began, isn't it."

"I believe so. I just called Paige. She's coming over with her sister and nephew. I think, if you come as well, the three of us should be able to explain what we've just experienced to the others."

Epilogue

B EFORE the plague hit the earth, Greg Davenport had been without a
job for almost a month. He had placed his resume online in an effort
to find a job. Shortly after the plague hit, there were several offers for him
to choose from. One job that got his attention was with the government to
help in the recovery efforts. Greg thought that being a government employee would be a good option, so he took the job offer. During his orientation,
he learned that the recovery job was to go to abandoned homes looking for
bodies. In the end it wasn't a recovery effort as much as it was a cleanup
effort.

Now just a month after the plague, he found himself going through
neighborhoods knocking on doors. If no one answered his knock, his job
was to get into the house to see if any bodies needed to be taken care of.

When he first found out what the job would entail, he considered
walking away and looking for another job. Then he thought about the
families of these people who might not even know that their loved one had
passed away. He was also told that when this task was complete, he would
be guaranteed a promotion.

It was a miserable job because the bodies he found had been there
for a month and were in decomposition. Thankfully he was provided a
HAZMAT suit. His job was to go and find the bodies and then radio in
the address and how many bodies needed to be taken care of. Greg was
provided with a small SUV that was bright green with large block letters
in white that read RECOVERY UNIT. Driving a vehicle that was so plainly
marked turned out to be helpful. People in the communities recognized the

SUV and would go out to him and point out the homes that were suspicious to them. Nine times out of ten their directions were accurate.

Most of the bodies he found were in their beds, which made sense because the plague had hit around the middle of the night in the U.S. and most people just died in their sleep. Because they had been dead for a month and because of the plague's effects on the body, the bodies had begun to liquefy and would be unrecognizable to any of their families.

One difference he found was when he came to a home in Avondale, Georgia. When he got there, the first thing he noticed was that there were several cars in the driveway. That made him think that there must have been some sort of party going on when the plague hit. When he entered the home, he found the bodies almost immediately, and none of them were in bed. He found all of the bodies in the dining room. They seemed to have been sitting around the table. He counted six adults and one child. One thing that stood out to him was a neatly stacked ream of paper in the center of the table with a post-it note on top. The note said, "We didn't die. Please study this."

Up until this day, Greg had never taken anything out of a home where he had found victims of the plague. This time his curiosity took over and he picked up the stack of paper. He walked out to his truck and radioed in the address along with the number of bodies. Then he marked the house by putting what looked like green crime scene tape across the front door along with a sticker on the door that had his I.D. number on it. Having done this, he proceeded to the other houses in the neighborhood.

When the end of the workday came, Greg drove back to the garage to turn in his truck and equipment to be cleaned. Before turning in his keys, he removed the ream of paper and placed it in his personal vehicle. Then he showered and put on his street clothes before driving back to his apartment.

Greg knew that he would be fired instantly if it was found out that he had taken this from the house. Not only was the policy set up to discourage stealing, he had been instructed it was also used as a measure to try and keep contaminants from spreading. He couldn't resist taking it, though, after seeing the message on the post-it note. That short message told him that somehow these people knew that the plague was about to hit.

"The first question you are probably asking yourself is how did we know this plague was about to hit when no one else did."

From there it went on to tell the story of three people. Two of them worked as EMT's with an ambulance service, and the third was a columnist. Although the men knew each other from work their lives had never crossed paths with the girl who was the columnist. It went on to tell in detail what happened shortly after the plague. Greg was familiar with some of those details, and others he made a mental note to check out. The story continued, telling about things that hadn't happened yet. If it weren't for this part of the story, Greg would have considered this some sort of elaborate practical joke. The story concluded by making a very bold statement saying the people who are now gone were not victims of a plague, but they were born again believers who had been called home by God.

At that point, Greg got up and walked away from the pages, determined not to waste any more of his time reading a bunch of junk like that. He went to his coffee maker and made himself a cup of coffee. Then went to his living room, turning on the TV to watch a show that was about to start. The show was a drama series and in this episode one of the main characters was going through a spirituality crisis. After the show was over, Greg went to the kitchen to make himself something to eat. Walking by the kitchen table with the pages on it, he glanced at them and made the decision to leave them there and eat in the living room. After dinner he watched one more show and then went to bed.

The next day was a typical workday for Greg, checking out the houses in the surrounding area. All day he never saw another package like the one he had found the day before. Even though he tried, he just could not get the story he had read out of his mind. When the day was over, he just couldn't resist going back to reading it again. On a whim, he went to a bookstore and bought a Bible on his way home. He had never read the Bible before, but he was sure that, given some time, he would be able to work it out.

Greg spent the next two weeks studying the information in the stack of paper as well as the Bible he bought. In the end, he knew that what he was reading was true. The message that was left by those people gave him a sense of hope.

"If you know in your heart that God has called his children home, then what do you do with that knowledge? We believe that God gave us the vision that we have shared with you for more than one reason. First, it was for us to come to a saving knowledge of Jesus Christ. We believe that another reason was for us to share this information with others. The next seven years are

going to be very difficult, and you may not survive. If you will hold tightly to the truth you now know, you will spend eternity with the Father."

www.ingramcontent.com/pod-product-compliance
Lightning Source LLC
Chambersburg PA
CBHW070039030726
47506CB00003B/807

* 9 7 8 1 6 6 6 7 3 6 3 6 6 *